THE GLADIATOR THIEF

Jeffrey Stoy

For my incredible family, thank you for letting me turn every family dinner into a story meeting and for pretending to be fascinated when I explained every single detail.
You deserve medals... or at least pizza.

CONTENTS

PROLOGUE: THE ECHO OF MAUI

The waves of Maui still echoed in Jack Sawyer's mind.

Even now, months later, he could close his eyes and hear them, steady, powerful, unpredictable. The same way every mystery seemed to start. It had begun with the "Young Innovators Fair", a trip that was supposed to be about science, technology, and maybe a few new friends. Instead, it had turned into an adventure that changed everything. He and Naomi Tanaka had uncovered a conspiracy involving missing technology, hidden labs, and a man whose genius had nearly cost lives. They'd faced danger, solved riddles, and somehow made it out alive.

Back home in Mill Bay, life had returned to normal. Jack had finally passed his driving test completed the safety course and road test for his motorcycle license, too. It felt like another small step toward independence. He had dreams of getting his own car if he could get a summer job and save some more money. He had used the $5,000 grant he received from his winnings in Maui to finish his reading app and get it in the market. He priced it as low as he could ($1 per download) so it could be used by anyone. He had a small stream of royalties coming in but it wasn't enough to buy a car.

At least, that's what everyone thought.

Jack had built a small detective office in his backyard The Mill Bay Detective Agency from scrap wood, old nails, and a stubborn sense that the world still held too many secrets. It was nearly ready to open to the public. Reading and writing his business plan for his little office had taken him longer than he'd admit. Dyslexia still made reading slow needing his full concentration, but he'd learned to see patterns in the confusion, to find meaning where others saw disorder. Maybe that was why he was good at solving mysteries: the world's chaos just looked like another code waiting to be cracked. Every plank reminded him of Maui: of decoding encrypted files, of chasing answers through tropical forests, and of standing side by side with Naomi when the truth finally came crashing down.

But the quiet didn't last.

Jack had promised his dad he'd take it easy, focus on school, basketball, and "stay out of trouble for at least one semester." But normal life never fit him for long. Mysteries had a way of finding him or maybe he had a way of finding them.

He didn't know yet that his next case would begin not with a science fair or a secret lab, but with a movie ticket. And that somewhere between the blinding lights of fame and the shadows behind the cameras, another mask was waiting to be lifted. Because for Jack Sawyer, solving mysteries wasn't just a hobby anymore. It was who he was.

CHAPTER 1: A DOUBLE-BUTTER POPCORN-SIZED OPPORTUNITY

Jack Sawyer sat at his desk in the Mill Bay Detective Agency, a compact greenhouse/tiny home he and his dad had built in the back corner of their yard.

Last year he'd cracked his first major case *The Maui Mystery* and his dad had said, "If you're going to be the town's go-to detective, you'll need an office as sharp as you are."

Now Jack leaned back in his chair, fingers hovering above the keyboard as he finished an email to Naomi Tanaka, his partner from that first case. Her updates always made him smile. She'd donated her ReefScan drone to a coral-reef preservation project "it felt right," she'd written, "like the drone finally found its true calling."

Naomi was juggling schoolwork and a new obsession: basketball. Your fault, she'd teased, blaming Jack's endless pickup games. He admired that about her; Naomi never eased into anything; she dove straight in. She'd was working evenings and weekends as an investigative journalist with an International Media Company based on Maui.

Jack hit "send" and wondered if she'd ever visit Mill Bay. If she did, he knew they'd stumble onto another mystery before the day was out.

At six-foot-three, Jack's head nearly brushed the doorway as he stepped outside. His lean, athletic build came from hours on the basketball court as Mill Bay High's star forward, but it was his messy brown hair and sharp brown eyes that gave him away, a mind always solving something.

From the porch of his tiny office he could just see Lake Naismith glinting through the trees. Down by the dock his younger sister, Georgia, was coaxing their tortoise Pippin along with a handful of lettuce and dandelions, walking him like a dog with all the patience in the world.

Their house sat at the far end of a quiet cul-de-sac, perched above the lake. The yard sloped to Skeleton Cove, a treacherous inlet where dark currents once dragged stray logs and sometimes unlucky men under. The abandoned mill still stood nearby, a ghost of timber and glass guarding the shore. Against that backdrop the Sawyers' two-storey home glowed with wide windows and warm light.

Adventure seemed to live in the backyard itself: the

detective shed crouched among the trees, and the rocky shoreline still whispered stories of the cove's past.

Today, though, there was no case to solve and no practice to make. Just a normal outing with his best friend.
Or as Jack had learned, as normal as anything could be when Anthony was involved.

"Jack! Let's go! We're gonna miss the previews!"
Anthony's voice rang from the driveway, full of urgency. He was practically bouncing on his toes, curls flopping as he waved his phone. The logo of *Gladiator Uprising* blazed across his T-shirt.

"I'm coming, I'm coming," Jack called, locking the door. "You're more hyped than a kid on Christmas morning."

"Are you kidding?" Anthony's eyes were wide with excitement. "It's not just a movie — it's the movie. *Gladiator Uprising* is the event of the year. People say it's even better than the last two!"

The franchise's star, Darius Slate, wasn't much older than they were, which still amazed them. Barely out of high school, he'd gone from local theatre to world fame almost overnight. With his chiseled jaw, piercing blue eyes, and easy charisma, he seemed born for the role of Myron, the farmer who became a legend. Jack admired him, though he wondered what kind of pressure came with fame that fast.

Anthony kept talking as they walked, and Jack

couldn't help smiling. His friend's excitement was infectious. He wasn't as obsessed with the franchise, but the story's mix of underdog grit and epic battles was hard not to love.

By the time they reached the Mill Bay Theatre, the sidewalks were packed with fans in gladiator helmets, capes, and foam swords. Chatter buzzed through the warm evening like static.

"Think about it," Anthony said, weaving through the crowd. "One day people might dress up as you: Jack Sawyer, the Mill Bay Detective."

Jack laughed. "I'm pretty sure Georgia and Pippin have a better shot at that."

Outside the theatre a towering cardboard standee of *Gladiator Uprising*: Rise of the Myrmidons loomed over the doors — Myron in full armour, sword raised amid flames. Anthony snapped a selfie beside it before pulling Jack toward the lobby.

Inside, the air smelled of butter and excitement. Fans crowded the concession lines, and a popcorn machine rattled nonstop. Then Jack spotted a bright poster near the counter:

WIN A CHANCE TO TRAIN AT THE *GLADIATOR ACADEMY* AND BE AN EXTRA IN THE NEXT MOVIE!
Underneath, a QR code.

Anthony froze. "Jack… do you see this?"

"Oh, I see it," Jack said.

"This is destiny." Anthony already had his phone out. "Trivia contest? Please. I was born for this."

"You realize the odds are, like, one in a million," Jack said, though he knew logic never slowed Anthony down.

"It's not about odds. It's about faith."
He scanned the code and dove into the quiz.

The movie was everything the hype promised — epic battles, heartbreak, triumph. Anthony mouthed half the lines; Jack found himself leaning forward anyway, caught in the story. When the final fight erupted, the crowd cheered as if they were inside the arena.

As the credits rolled, Anthony's phone buzzed. He glanced down and froze.

"Jack," he whispered.

"What?"

"I... I won." His hands shook as he turned the screen.

CONGRATULATIONS! YOU'VE WON A TRIP TO THE *GLADIATOR ACADEMY*! BRING A FRIEND TO TRAIN AS A GLADIATOR AND BE AN EXTRA IN THE NEXT MOVIE!

Jack blinked. "No way."

"YES WAY!" Anthony shouted, jumping to his feet. Heads turned, but he didn't care. He grabbed Jack by the shoulders and shook him. "We're going! *Gladiator Academy*! You and me!"

By the time they reached the lobby his phone was already pinging with congratulations from half of Mill Bay.

After the commotion they stopped for pizza at the Tiki Club, the lakeside hub where Jack's parents were members. The scent of wood-fired dough and garlic filled the air; laughter rolled between the tables.
Jack spotted their friends Anna and Bennett in a booth. Anna's baseball cap was pushed back over her ponytail, she'd clearly just finished a shift working in the restaurant, and Bennett was already talking soccer.

"Here's to the luckiest guy in Mill Bay," Jack said, clapping Anthony on the back. "Future *Gladiator Academy* star."

Anna raised her soda. "Congrats! Just don't trip over your own sword."

Bennett grinned. "If they need a soccer-playing gladiator, I'm available."

Anthony puffed up theatrically. "Thank you, thank you! You're all looking at the future face of *Gladiator Uprising*."

They laughed and clinked glasses. As they tore into the pizza, Jack looked at his friends, Anna's speed, Bennett's energy, Anthony's enthusiasm and pictured them all in armour, shoulder to shoulder in some sun-lit arena.
The thought made him grin.

Something told him that whatever awaited at *Gladiator Academy* would be unforgettable — and maybe a little too real.

CHAPTER 2: AMONG GLADIATORS

The final days of school flew by tests, locker cleanouts, endless talk of summer plans. For Jack and Anthony, everything revolved around the Academy. By the last bell, their duffel bags were packed: sneakers, notebooks, and the "lucky" gladiator trinkets Anthony refused to leave behind.

The real adventure and maybe their biggest mystery yet was about to begin.

The *Gladiator Academy* was everything Jack and Anthony had imagined and more.
Built on a sprawling studio lot just outside Mill Bay, it looked as if it had been lifted straight from the *Gladiator Uprising* movies. A massive colosseum-style arena dominated the grounds, its stone façade throwing long shadows across a maze of smaller buildings, barracks for extras, a gym packed with weights, and a costume workshop where racks of glittering armor gleamed under the lights.

"Dude, this is unreal," Anthony whispered as they passed beneath a towering archway carved with the Myrmidon crest. "It's like stepping into the movie."

Jack nodded, trying to take it all in. He wasn't as starstruck as Anthony, but even he couldn't deny how impressive it was. The air smelled of fresh-cut wood from the props workshop, mixed with the metallic tang of sweat from the training grounds. Around them, other contest winners and hopeful extras wandered wide-eyed, soaking in the atmosphere.

They were met by a man who could have been cast in the movie himself. Scott Myller, a grizzled stunt coordinator with shoulders like a battering ram and a voice built for command.

"Welcome to *Gladiator Academy*," he barked, pacing before the group. "You're here because someone thinks you've got what it takes to step into a gladiator's sandals. But let's be clear, this isn't cosplay, and it's not a theme park. If you want to be an extra in *Gladiator Uprising*, you're going to earn it. We'll train for the next week and then decide what part you can play."

Jack exchanged a glance with Anthony, who was practically vibrating with excitement.

Scott clapped his hands, and a group of trainers stepped forward, all muscle, scars, and swagger. "You'll be learning from the best stunt team in the business," he continued. "We'll teach you to fight, fall, and make it look good. But first, we'll see if you've got the grit to survive the basics."

The "basics" turned out to be brutal.

They started with conditioning drills that left Jack's legs burning and Anthony gasping for air. Then came weapon training, wooden swords, blocks, parries, and precision strikes. Jack quickly realized there was an art to it: every swing calculated to look dangerous without actually landing a hit.

"Keep your guard up, Sawyer!" Scott barked as Jack stumbled on a feint. A wooden blade cracked against his shin, and he winced.

"Easy for you to say," Jack muttered, resetting his stance.

Anthony, meanwhile, was in heaven. "Did you see that? I just nailed the Myrmidon sweep!" he shouted, nearly clipping Jack's shoulder with his overenthusiastic swing.

"Yeah," Jack grumbled, ducking, "and you almost took my head off."

The footwork drills were relentless, but Jack's basketball instincts gave him an edge. His balance, timing, and quick pivots made him a natural at dodging blows. By the end of the morning session, even Scott seemed impressed.

"Not bad, Sawyer," he said gruffly. "You've got good instincts. Remind me to put you up front when we run formations."

Jack didn't think much of it until later, when a woman from the production crew, headset, clipboard, the works, lingered nearby during their break.

"You two keep this up," she said, gesturing at Jack's precision and Anthony's flair, "and we might have bigger plans for you than background roles. Finish the Academy, and we'll talk."

Anthony's jaw dropped. Jack just raised an eyebrow.

"Guess we'd better make it through," Jack said, smirking.

"Oh, we're making it through," Anthony replied, grinning.

By midday, Jack was drenched in sweat and questioning his life choices until they reached the colosseum stage.

The trainers demonstrated a mock battle that was pure movie magic: swords clashed, fighters leaped, and every fall looked painfully real. Jack couldn't look away. Every motion told a story, triumph, fear, defiance.

When it ended, Scott faced the group. "That's what we're aiming for," he said. "It's not enough to fight, you have to perform. Every swing, every stumble, every victory has to mean something. You're not extras. You're gladiators."

Later, Jack and Anthony collapsed onto a bench near the edge of the training ground.

"That was insane," Anthony said, still grinning through the dirt and sweat.

"Insane is one word for it," Jack said, gulping water. His muscles ached, his hands were raw, and he loved every second. Around him, armor gleamed, the colosseum loomed, and trainees pushed themselves past exhaustion.

This wasn't a fan contest anymore. It was a challenge and Jack never backed away from a challenge.

"Ready to go again tomorrow?" Anthony asked.

Jack smirked. "Bring it on."

By the third day, they were summoned to a meeting with Scott and several producers. Jack wiped the sweat from his forehead as they stepped into the room.

"You've impressed us," Scott said, his tone gruff but approving. "You've got what it takes to be more than extras."

A producer added, clipboard in hand, "We're inviting you both to return next week for six weeks of training and filming. You'll train harder, but you'll have speaking parts."

Jack and Anthony stared at each other, speechless.

For the first time, it felt real, Jack and Anthony weren't just trainees anymore. They were on the payroll. Every stunt, every rehearsal, every long day would come with an actual paycheck attached, something that made Anthony grin like he'd already won an Oscar.

Scott's smirk widened. "Anthony, you'll join Darius Slate's Myrmidons. Jack, with your height and presence, you'll play his lead opponent the enemy gladiator. Darius's rival in the arena."

Anthony's smile stretched ear to ear. Jack just nodded, feeling the adrenaline spike.

Not long after, Scott pulled Jack aside. "You'll be a Retiarius," he explained, handing him a trident and a weighted net. "Sea gladiator. Perfect for your build. You're Myron's nemesis the ocean's power against the empire's discipline."

Jack hefted the trident, feeling its weight. "Nice," he said, imagining the weapon flashing under the arena lights.

Scott demonstrated a sweeping motion. "Your reach gives you the advantage. Control the space. Keep Myron on the defensive."

Jack grinned, picturing the duel already. His costume, Scott explained, would include leather straps lined with seashells, a scaled breastplate like fish armor, and a dark, wave-like cape. The thought made Jack's imagination fill with images of him being a hero.

The weeks ahead were going to be unforgettable.

CHAPTER 3: THE FIRST STRIKE

The quiet town of Mill Bay erupted in excitement when Darius Slate, the star of *Gladiator Uprising*, arrived with an entourage fit for royalty.

The small Canadian city nestled in the Rocky Mountains was an unlikely location for a Hollywood production but one of the producers was from the area and was able to get the production moved there to be closer to home and to save money.

A convoy of black SUVs rolled through town, flanked by trucks carrying gym equipment, designer furniture, and even a portable espresso bar. Darius had taken over an entire airport hangar to store his private jet and the overflow of luxury cars, motorcycles, and boats. The five-star hotel on the edge of town was booked exclusively for his team of stylists, trainers, assistants, and security.

Rumour spread fast. Darius was expected to visit the *Gladiator Academy* by the end of the week to meet the trainees and oversee rehearsals but for now, he was busy settling into his temporary kingdom.

According to whispers, he'd even tried to visit the

Tiki Club after hearing about its exclusivity and great pizza, only to be turned away for lack of a member sponsor, a rare rejection for Hollywood's newest golden boy.

His arrival made the town feel suddenly smaller, and to Jack and Anthony, it was a reminder that they'd stepped into a world far bigger than Mill Bay.

The buzz of the *Gladiator Academy* filled every hour, the clash of wooden swords, the bark of instructors, the thud of feet on packed sand. But even amid the noise, Jack began to sense something different in the air.

Whispers rippled among the trainers. Glances darted between phones. And then there was Mia Calderon, a production assistant who stood apart from the chaos.

Where most assistants looked frazzled, Mia moved with quiet precision, clipboard tucked under her arm, green eyes sharp and steady. Her red hair gleamed under the sun as she crossed the yard, her calm confidence making her seem… different. More in control.

Jack found himself watching her almost as much as he watched the stunt team.

"Something's up," he told Anthony one morning as they grabbed breakfast in the cafeteria. The room buzzed with chatter, but Jack's focus stayed fixed on a group of trainers huddled near the door, whispering.

"Probably just studio drama," Anthony said through a mouthful of toast. "Maybe they ran out of fake blood."

Jack rolled his eyes, though his gut told him otherwise.

That afternoon, during a break, his suspicions sharpened. He passed by Mia, who was studying a tablet. A headline flashed across the screen:

"Bank Robber Strikes Again — In Gladiator Armor!"

Jack's curiosity spiked. "Mind if I take a look?"

Mia hesitated, then shrugged. "It's all over the news. Crazy, right?"

Jack tried to read quickly. He squinted at the article, rereading the same paragraph for the third time. The words still tangled in his brain, but he'd learned to slow down, to find the rhythm hidden between the sentences. Dyslexia had taught him patience, and patience was a detective's best weapon. The robbery had taken place downtown the night before. Witnesses claimed the thief wore full gladiator armor, helmet, sword, and all and fought off guards with skill that seemed cinematic. He'd escaped on a motorcycle with a bag of cash.

"The guy's movements were perfect," one witness said. "Like something out of a movie."

Jack handed the tablet back, his mind racing. The fighting style, the precision, it was too familiar. It sounded exactly like the choreography they'd been learning at the Academy.

That evening, Jack found Anthony sitting on the bench near the edge of the training grounds.

"A bank robber dressed as a gladiator?" Anthony repeated, incredulous. "You're kidding."

"I'm serious," Jack said. "The way they described it it's like something one of the stunt guys could pull off."

Anthony shook his head. "Come on. Why would anyone here risk everything to rob a bank? There are easier ways to make money."

"Maybe," Jack said, "but think about it, who else has access to movie-quality armor and knows how to use it?"

Anthony frowned, his usual spark dimming. "You really think it could be someone from the Academy?"

"I don't know," Jack admitted, staring at the sky. "But it's too weird to ignore. Let's just keep an eye out and see if anyone's acting off."

The next day, the robbery was all anyone could talk about. Trainers whispered between sessions. Crew members looked tense. Only Mia seemed unfazed, striding through the set like nothing had changed. That calm confidence again, or was it something else?

Jack couldn't tell if she was fearless or hiding

something. Either way, he decided to watch her closely.

Among the Myrmidons, one fighter stood out—not because he was the fastest or strongest, but because he didn't quite fit. Broderick Johnson was older than most of the trainees, his movements rougher, more mechanical. A jagged scar ran along his jaw, and his eyes carried the wary alertness of someone who'd seen more real fights than staged ones.

"That's Broderick," Anthony whispered beside Jack. "Used to work security before he joined the stunt team. Word is, he's got a temper."

Jack watched as Broderick missed a cue and slammed his shield against the ground hard enough to make the instructor flinch. The man muttered an apology, but Jack caught the way his jaw tightened.

"He doesn't seem like the 'team player' type," Jack said quietly.

Anthony shrugged. "Maybe he just takes it seriously."

But as Broderick stalked off toward the locker tents, Jack couldn't shake a prickling unease. There was something about the man's precision, the way he carried himself, like a soldier who hadn't quite left the battlefield behind.

During sparring, his distraction earned him a sharp rebuke.

"Focus, Sawyer!" Scott barked as Jack fumbled a

block. "You won't survive the arena daydreaming."

Jack gritted his teeth and swung back into rhythm, but his mind wouldn't settle. Somewhere behind the shining props and choreographed battles, real danger was lurking.

That night, Jack sat on his bunk, scrolling through notes on his phone a habit left over from his time in Maui. He listed every detail from the article, matching it with what he'd noticed around the Academy.

Anthony appeared at the doorway, holding two sodas. "You're not gonna drop this, are you?"

Jack shook his head. "If someone here's involved, I need to know."

Anthony sighed, handing him a can. "Fine. But if this gets us kicked out, you're explaining it to my parents."

Jack grinned. "Deal."

Still, even as they joked, the question haunted him: Who at the Academy could be the Gladiator Thief?

Training ramped up the next morning. Scott put Jack through trident drills before sunrise. The weapon was heavier than it looked, demanding a perfect balance of strength and timing.

"It's all about rhythm," Scott barked. "Your trident's an extension of you. Control the distance. Miss once, and you're finished."

Jack's early attempts were clumsy, more knots than net but by midweek, he'd found his rhythm. His basketball footwork translated perfectly. He struck, spun, and cast his net in one fluid motion.

For the first time, he felt like a real gladiator.

Across the arena, Anthony and the twenty Myrmidon trainees drilled sword formations with military precision. "You're not solo fighters," Scott reminded them. "You're a legion. You move as one."

The group advanced in tight formation, shields locking with a satisfying clatter. Anthony couldn't resist adding his trademark flair, spinning and flourishing to mixed reactions from the trainers.

"Save it for the cameras," one muttered.

Still, by the end of each session, the Myrmidons moved like a single force, and Anthony thrived on it.

But even in formation, one space was always left open, the spot reserved for Darius Slate himself.

The trainers insisted there was no need to worry. "Slate's been through this three times," Scott said. "He knows the routines better than anyone. He'll join you when he's ready."

Still, Jack couldn't shake the feeling that the star's absence was strange.

If Darius was the heart of the production… why wasn't he training with them?

CHAPTER 4: TRAINING IN SHADOWS

The morning air buzzed with anticipation as Scott Myller gathered the trainees in the main arena.

"Listen up," he barked, his sharp voice slicing through the chatter. "We're almost a third of the way through the schedule and will finish up training and get to filming what we've been working on. The Myrmidons are beginning specialized training sessions effective immediately. They've got stunt work to refine, so they'll be training separately for the rest of the week."

Jack forced a smile, but unease tugged at him. Something about the Myrmidons didn't sit right.

Later that day, Jack found Mia Calderon in the props room, the same assistant who'd shared her tablet earlier. Her red hair was pulled back into a neat ponytail, and her green eyes darted between props with laser focus. Freckles dusted her nose and cheeks; her headset and clipboard completed the picture of quiet authority. Amid the constant clatter of crew and equipment, she moved like someone who thrived in chaos.

"Hey, Mia," Jack said.

"Back again?" she asked, glancing up with a teasing smirk. "What is it this time, Sawyer?"

Jack scratched the back of his neck. "Something like that. I was wondering if I could take a quick look at the stunt crew profiles. I've been thinking about expanding my training, and I want to see who's got the skills I could learn from."

Her eyebrow lifted, but she didn't seem suspicious. "All right, but don't tell anyone I let you peek behind the curtain."

She passed him her tablet. Jack scrolled through the list of names and bios, fighters, gymnasts, and martial artists. The Myrmidons' files stood out: nearly identical builds, matching measurements, and uncanny similarities in background.

"Twins," Jack muttered, spotting a pair of brothers. "And triplets? Seriously?"

"Yeah," Mia said, leaning over his shoulder. "If you want a seamless unit on screen, starting with people who already move alike makes sense."

Jack nodded but kept scrolling. Some files were curiously incomplete, missing credits, vague stunt certifications, blank sections where recent work should have been.

"Why are some of these so vague?" he asked.

"Could be nothing," Mia replied. "Could be studio politics. Stuff gets lost when we're running on tight deadlines."

"Right," Jack said, but unease prickled at the back of his mind.

That evening, while stretching in the dorms, Jack confided in Anthony.

"Something about the Myrmidons doesn't sit right," he said quietly.

"You're still on that?" Anthony sighed. "Jack, they're elite stunt performers. What could possibly be wrong with that?"

Jack hesitated. "They're too similar. And the studio's going out of its way to keep them apart from everyone else."

Anthony shook his head, unconvinced. Jack didn't press. He knew how much Anthony idolized the group and Darius Slate.

As the week wore on, Jack kept watching. He saw Myrmidons leaving the lot midday on motorcycles, disappearing for hours. They rarely talked to other trainees. Even off the clock, their movements were synchronized, deliberate, and rehearsed.

Every new detail deepened the chill in Jack's gut. The Myrmidons and maybe the Academy itself were hiding something.

By midweek, the tension broke with Darius Slate's arrival.

Clad in a sleek version of Myrmidon armour, cape flowing behind him, the star strode into the arena like he owned it. His hair was perfect; his confidence filled the space. The Myrmidons snapped to attention as he passed, movements tightening under his gaze. Without a word, Darius took command, running them through complex formations with crisp authority.

Jack watched from the sidelines. Anthony, now one of them, followed Darius's cues with unshakable enthusiasm. The other trainees stared in awe. For most, it was a dream to see the franchise's hero up close.

For Jack, it only made the pit in his stomach grow.

That night, cross-legged on his bunk, Jack scrolled through articles on his laptop. Each robbery had followed the same formula: daring, theatrical, executed with precision. The thief wore gladiator armour and escaped on a motorcycle.

But what really caught Jack's attention was the timeline.

The first heist had happened only weeks after production started on the original *Gladiator Uprising*. Every new film had been followed by another wave of robberies each one more elaborate than the last.

Coincidence? Or someone on the inside using movie training for real-world crimes?

Jack leaned back, thinking fast. He needed Mia's help, someone with access to past crew lists, especially people tied to the stunt department and armoury.

But for now, morning would come too soon. He shut his laptop, the blue glow fading.

If the Gladiator Thief was connected to the Academy, then he was closer to the truth than he realized.

And one wrong move could make him the next target.

The heat rose off the arena sand in shimmering waves, and even the fake Roman columns looked like they were melting. Jack and Mia sat on the edge of the bleachers, his helmet tossed aside, and her tablet dropped at her feet, unwrapping their energy bars like survivors rationing supplies.

"So," Mia said, squinting toward the Myrmidons zipping around the set on black motorcycles, "why do stuntmen need to practice formation riding for a movie set entirely in ancient Rome?"

Jack took a long drink from his water bottle. "Because apparently the Myrmidons fight traffic before they fight gladiators."

She smirked. "Seems efficient."

"Yeah, if the movie was Fast and Furious: Coliseum Drift."

Mia laughed, shaking her head. "You know, for a guy who almost passed out during warm-ups, you're getting funnier."

"It's a survival mechanism," Jack said. "If I don't joke, I'll realize how much my legs hurt."

She nudged him with her elbow. "You'll live. You did better today."

"Thanks," he said. "I've been trying not to fall on my face in front of the girl who actually reads the manual."

Mia laughed, brushing a loose strand of red hair from her face. For a moment, the two sat in easy silence, watching sunlight glint off the armor racks and the motorcycles circling the practice ring.

"You know," she said finally, "for all the sweat and blisters, this might actually be fun."

Jack grinned. "Don't say that too loud. They'll make us do another week."

"Then I'll deny everything," she said, smiling back.

The director's whistle shrieked across the arena, and the Myrmidons revved their bikes again. Jack groaned, pushing to his feet.

"Back to pretending we know what we're doing?" Mia asked.

"Story of my life," Jack replied, offering her a hand.

She took it, her grip firm but warm. For just a second, the roar of engines and the glare of the sun faded away, leaving only the two of them—and the faint sense that something real was starting to spark between them.

CHAPTER 5: THE GLADIATOR MASK

The day started like any other at *Gladiator Academy*, the clang of swords, the bark of instructors, the echo of combat drills rolling across the lot.

Jack had just finished a round of trident exercises when his phone buzzed. He wiped the sweat from his brow, checked the screen and froze.

"Gladiator Thief Strikes Again: Another Daring Bank Heist in Mill Bay!"

His pulse spiked as he tapped the alert.

The article described a thief in full gladiator armour storming a downtown bank, moving with such precision and grace that witnesses called it "almost choreographed."

Security footage showed the figure disarming a guard with a clean shield swipe, spinning clear, and vanishing on a sleek black motorcycle.

But what caught Jack's attention most came later in the broadcast commentary.

Analysts debated how the thief's ornate helmet made them virtually unidentifiable, its design theatrical, intimidating, and oddly cinematic.

"The Gladiator Mask is a perfect disguise," one anchor said.

"It hides identity and enhances the spectacle. Witnesses focus on the drama instead of the details. It's genius."

"Or rehearsed," Jack muttered, unease coiling tight in his chest.

That afternoon, training hit full swing, but Jack couldn't unsee the parallels.

One of their drills involved an upward shield swipe followed by a pivoting spin, exactly the move described in the report.

Every step of the Myrmidons' routine matched the thief's precision: the disarms, the acrobatics, the flow.

Watching them was like watching the crime itself replayed at half-speed.

Their motions were too smooth, too perfect and more like a performance than a practice.

Anthony, newly embedded among them, looked exhilarated.

When Jack voiced his concern later, Anthony just laughed.

"They're stunt guys, Jack. Their job is to look choreographed."

"Yeah," Jack said quietly, "that's what worries me."

That evening, Jack tracked down Mia Calderon.

She was in the props room again, lining up a row of helmets identical to the one the thief had worn.

"Mia," he said, stepping through the doorway, "got a minute?"

She looked up from her clipboard, smirking. "Another favour?"

Jack grinned faintly. "Not quite. I've got questions about the props, specifically the Myrmidon gear."

Mia crossed her arms. "All right, shoot."

"Is there a record of the old props? From the first *Gladiator Uprising*?"

Mia snorted. "Officially, yes. Realistically? No. The old gear was 'retired,' but no one actually tracked it. Some pieces went to crew, some to storage and some just disappeared. Why?"

Jack pulled out his phone and showed her the article. "The thief's armour. The movements. It's not random it's trained. It's ours."

Her expression shifted from teasing to serious. "You think it's someone from the Academy?"

"Maybe someone who used to be," Jack said. "How many Myrmidons have there been, total?"

Mia sighed, scrolling through her tablet. "Seventy-three. Darius brings in new blood for every film, guys like Anthony, so they can blend in with the veterans."

Jack raised an eyebrow. "That's seventy-three people

with access to the armour and training."

"Exactly," Mia said. "And it doesn't stop there. Darius has this branding thing; he gives every Myrmidon a motorcycle to 'match the aesthetic.' They all get the same regimen: stunt fighting, precision riding, the works. By the time a film wraps, they're practically interchangeable."

She hesitated. "A lot of the earlier guys started their own stunt schools. Most kept their costumes, souvenirs, teaching tools, whatever. Now they're scattered everywhere."

Jack's mind raced. "So, the thief could be one of the current Myrmidons or someone from the earlier films who still has their gear."

"Exactly. And with how similar they look in uniform, good luck telling who's who."

That night, Jack sat in the blue glow of his laptop, piecing it all together.
The timeline, the choreography, the motorcycles, it all pointed back to the Myrmidons. But seventy-plus suspects across four movies and a dozen studios made it almost impossible to narrow down.

He jotted a note: Ask Mia about continuous crew access to costume, stunt, and prop departments.

But exhaustion won out. He leaned back against his pillow, eyes heavy. Somewhere out there, the Gladiator Thief was turning their movie training into a weapon and Jack was determined to unmask them before they struck again.

By the next morning, anticipation pulsed through the Academy.

It was nearly halfway through the summer. A week of bruises, drills, and endless choreography had pushed everyone to the edge. Scott and his training team was packing up to leave the academy and let the filming team take over.

Anthony was electric, thrilled to be sharing scenes with the Myrmidons and Darius Slate.

Jack tried to match his friend's excitement, but unease still tugged at him. The thief's shadow loomed large behind every flash of metal.

The Academy announced a surprise addition to the schedule: motorcycle drills. Officially, they were meant to help the Myrmidons improve "mobility and coordination," but everyone knew the truth. The motorcycles had nothing to do with *Gladiator Uprising*, and everything to do with being part of the Myrmidons. The rumble of engines echoed through the lot each morning, a ritual that felt more like an initiation than a rehearsal.

Jack watched from the sidelines as Anthony practiced tight cornering, the Myrmidons weaving through cones with near-military precision. "This isn't stunt work," Jack muttered. "It's formation riding."

Jack was halfway through his protein bar when Mia slid into the seat across from him in the cafeteria.

Her clipboard was gone, a bad sign. She only showed up without it when something serious was brewing.

"You've got a problem," she said quietly.

Jack blinked. "If this is about the trident drills, Scott already yelled at me as he was packing up."

"Not that." She leaned in, voice low. "People are talking. About you."

"Me?"

"Yeah. Word's going around that you're poking into the robberies. And some of the stunt crew know about The Maui Mystery."

Jack froze. "How would they even?"

"Someone must've Googled you after the contest. You're not exactly anonymous anymore, Sawyer. Half the internet still calls you the kid detective who cracked that Maui tech scandal."

"Great," he muttered. "Exactly what I needed, celebrity status at *Gladiator Academy*."

Mia didn't smile. "It's not funny. The wrong people know. A couple of the Myrmidons were asking if you're 'investigating' the set."

Jack's stomach tightened. "So, they think I'm snooping?"

"No," she said. "They know you are. Whatever you did in Maui, it put a target on your back here. Just... be careful what questions you ask, okay?"

Jack exhaled slowly. "I can handle a few rumors."

"This isn't high-school gossip, Jack. These people guard secrets for a living." Her eyes searched his. "Next time you go chasing clues, make sure someone knows where you're going."

He gave a crooked grin. "So, you're volunteering?"

"I'm making sure you don't end up as the next missing prop," she said, standing. Then softer, "You've got instincts, Sawyer. Don't let them get you hurt."

She walked off before he could answer, leaving Jack staring at the half-finished protein bar.

For the first time, he realized the mystery wasn't just on set anymore it had found him.

That evening, as the sun dropped low, Jack caught up with Mia walking off set.
"You know," he said casually, "if you're staying in town for the weekend, you should swing by my place. It's right on the lake. We could stop by the Tiki Club; my parents are members."

Mia looked over, freckles glowing in the last light. "The Tiki Club? That's the one everyone talks about, right? Super exclusive?"

Jack shrugged. "Kinda. But if you know someone, it's not a big deal. And since you're not from Mill Bay, you've got to try it at least once."

Her smile turned genuine. "I might take you up on that. I could use a break. Balancing this internship with high school is rough."

Jack blinked. "Wait, you're still in high school?"

"Yup." She laughed softly. "It's part of a special program. I want to act someday, so working on this set feels like a dream, but it's intense. I'm still doing schoolwork over the summer to make sure I stay on track."

Jack nodded, recognizing the drive in her eyes. "Then you've earned some downtime. The lake, the Tiki Club, it's all pretty low-key, but it'll be fun."

For the first time in days, Jack felt his shoulders ease. Maybe, for one night, he could stop thinking like a detective.

Maybe he could just be a kid again—before the shadows crept back.

CHAPTER 6:
ARENA OF
DECEPTION

The weekend brought a much-needed break from the chaos of *Gladiator Academy* but for Jack Sawyer, the mystery of the Gladiator Thief only grew darker.

While most crew relaxed, Anthony was all in, devoting every spare hour to the Myrmidons. He'd mastered their motorcycle drills, perfecting the sharp, synchronized maneuvers that had become their trademark.

"Anthony's obsessed," Jack said as he sat on the dock beside Mia. Lake Naismith shimmered in the afternoon sun, but unease clouded his mood. "He's been texting me nonstop about how he nailed the formations. Apparently, Darius even complimented him."

Mia raised an eyebrow. "Formation riding? Sounds dramatic. Are you sure he's not just showing off?"

Jack smirked. "With Anthony? Always. But it fits. The Myrmidons are all about spectacle and honestly, it's like they're everywhere."

"Everywhere?" Mia asked, her green eyes narrowing with interest.

Jack nodded. "They're identical. It's like being trapped in a mirror maze they move the same, sound the same. You can't tell one from another. It's all designed that way. It's…" He paused, searching for the words. "An arena of deception. And I can't figure out how to see through it."

Mia tilted her head, thoughtful. "So, what's the next move? How do you find the person behind it?"

Jack hesitated. "There's one name I keep coming back to in the notes you provided: Marcus Trent. He was one of the original stunt coordinators for *Gladiator Uprising*, but he left the studio after a fight with the producers. He lives near here. If anyone knows what's really going on, it's him."

The next morning, Jack borrowed his parents' car, and he and Mia drove along the lake road, the early fog clinging to the trees. She ran her hand over the dashboard of the sporty convertible. "This is pretty nice for a high school student. How'd you end up with it?" Jack kept his eyes on the road but grimaced as he said, "It's my parents' car; I'm saving up for my own, I had to promise to take my sister to swimming lessons all next year and clean our tortoise's enclosure until Christmas just to get the keys a few times over the summer." Mia smiled as the hum of the engine filled the silence as Jack's mind turned over his suspicions again and again.

When they reached Marcus Trent's cabin, Jack wasn't sure what to expect. The place sat tucked among tall pines near a sports complex on the edge of town, motorcycle parts scattered across the yard. A half-finished bike gleamed beneath a tarp. On the porch, an old, weather-worn *Gladiator Uprising* poster flapped in the wind.

Mia gave a low whistle. "Definitely not living the Hollywood dream anymore."

Jack knocked. After a pause, the door creaked open and there he was. Marcus Trent. Broad shoulders, sharp eyes that missed nothing. Jack froze, his mind jolting at the sight. There was something hauntingly familiar about him.

"Who are you?" Marcus demanded.

"Jack Sawyer," Jack said, offering his hand. "This is Mia Calderon. We're from *Gladiator Academy*."

Marcus's expression darkened. "If this is about the studio, forget it. I'm done with that mess."

"It's not," Jack said quickly. "We're high school students and working on the new movie and heard you were a big part of the first movie and the specialist on everything Gladiator related. We just have a few questions."

Marcus hesitated, then stepped aside. "Fine. Come in."

Inside, the cabin was cluttered but organized, part

workshop, part museum. Tools lined the walls, and dusty props filled the shelves. A row of replica Myrmidon helmets sat on a workbench, their identical designs glinting faintly in the dim light.

"What do you want to know?" Marcus asked, crossing his arms.

Jack started with "What made you come up with the Myrmidons?"

Marcus's expression softened for a moment, a flicker of pride breaking through the weariness in his face. "The studio wanted soldiers who looked invincible —faceless, fearless, perfectly in sync. I pitched the Myrmidons as a unit that moved like a machine but performed like dancers. Every strike, every dodge, every movement was designed to look like art in motion." He gave a short, bitter laugh. "It worked. The audience loved them. But somewhere along the way, the studio forgot that behind every helmet was a real person who could get hurt."

He turned back toward the helmets, running a thumb across the edge of one. "We trained for months, timing, rhythm, precision. I designed the choreography myself. But Darius? He made it famous. He took my vision and turned it into a franchise." His jaw tightened.

Jack shifted uneasily, sensing the bitterness under Marcus's calm tone. "There's been a series of robberies," he said. "The thief's wearing gladiator armor. The moves and everything about it look choreographed. Like stunt work."

Marcus gave a dry laugh. "Wouldn't surprise me. Half the Myrmidons cared more about flash than safety. What's your point?"

Jack exchanged a glance with Mia. "We think someone from the original team might be involved. Someone who still has their gear or knows the routines."

Marcus's eyes narrowed. "Possible. The studio never tracked the props. And trust me, some of those guys were in it for the paycheck. If someone waved enough money, they'd jump."

"What about grudges?" Mia asked. "Anyone who might want payback?"

Marcus stiffened. "You think that's me?"

"No," Jack said, though his pulse quickened. "But you know how these stunts work. If someone wanted to turn them into crimes, how would they pull it off?"

Marcus sighed, running a hand through his hair. "Wouldn't be hard. The techniques are flashy, sure, but they're functional too. The armour's light. The helmets conceal your face. If you know the choreography and have the guts, yeah, you could rob a bank in full costume."

Jack studied him closely. The resemblance to Darius Slate was uncanny, the same jawline, the same presence. Even the cadence of his speech was familiar.

"You and Darius… you look a lot alike," Jack said carefully.

Marcus's mouth twitched into a wry smile. "Noticed that, huh? Darius and I go way back. I helped create the Myrmidon style, his fighting technique, his image, all of it. I trained him."

Jack's curiosity sharpened. "So why aren't you still involved?"

Marcus's expression hardened. "Creative differences," he said flatly. "Let's leave it there."

Jack and Mia asked a couple more questions, but Marcus had stopped giving more than one-word answers when the questions got too personal.

A few minutes later, Marcus had sent them out to the porch as he grabbed his phone to make a call. Jack "accidentally" dropped his keys bending low out of sight to pick them up. The metallic clatter echoed across the deck.

"Seriously?" Mia said, rolling her eyes.

"Guess I'm clumsy today," Jack muttered. "Go ahead, I'll catch up."

Mia headed for the car and Jack used the rattle of his keys as cover and he edged toward the side of the cabin, pressing himself against the wall. From inside, Marcus's voice carried clearly through the open window.

"I told you this would get messy!" he snapped.
A pause.

"No excuses. Now I've got kids snooping around asking questions."

Another pause. Then Marcus's voice dropped to a growl.

"You know what to do."

Jack's chest tightened. Every instinct screamed at him to run, but he forced himself to back away quietly, slipping his keys into his pocket as if nothing had happened.

By the time he reached the car, his expression was calm. His pulse was not.

"Everything okay?" Mia asked.

"Yeah," Jack said smoothly. "Let's just go."

On the drive back to Mill Bay, neither spoke for a long time. Finally, Mia broke the silence.

"Do you think he's telling the truth?"

Jack's knuckles whitened on the steering wheel. "Maybe. But he's hiding something. And if he really created Darius's whole Myrmidon persona, he might know more than he's admitting."

That night, Jack called Anna and Bennett. "I need a favor," he said, laying out what had happened.

"Stake him out?" Anna asked. "We can do that. But what are we watching for?"

"Anything suspicious," Jack said. "And if you can, get a photo or video. Just… be careful."

The next day, Anna and Bennett checked in.

Anna and Bennett had decided to follow Marcus after spotting him leaving on his motorcycle. They tailed him down the winding roads past the lake, Bennet's old car struggling to keep up with his speed. But Marcus rode like a ghost, cutting corners, vanishing behind turns, reappearing half a mile ahead before disappearing completely into the trees.

When they finally gave up and returned to Mill Bay, Bennett kicked at the gravel in frustration. "It's like he knew every shortcut before we even turned," he said.

Anna exhaled, glancing back toward the road. "No, he knew we were following him. He wanted us to lose him."

"Jack," Anna said, her voice low. "Marcus looks exactly like Darius Slate. It's eerie."

Bennett added, "They could be brothers. Same build, same voice. It's like Darius is a polished version of him."

Jack leaned back, his thoughts spinning. "If Marcus taught Darius everything he knows, and then got pushed out…"

Mia finished the thought. "He'd have motive. He'd know the moves. And he'd have the gear."

Jack nodded slowly, determination tightening his jaw. "Then we find out how deep this goes and whether Marcus Trent is the key to unmasking the Gladiator Thief."

Anna and Bennett agreed to keep tabs on Marcus

whenever they could. Their sports practices gave them a perfect excuse, their soccer and baseball fields were close to Trent's cabin, which people jokingly called his "unofficial *Gladiator Academy*."

Every few days, they'd meet Jack and Anthony over pizza at the Tiki Club, casually swapping updates while pretending to talk about the rest of their summer plans. Meanwhile, Jack, Mia, and Anthony dug into the current Myrmidons' backgrounds, cross-checking résumés, observing their behavior on set, and noting anyone whose past didn't quite line up.

It wasn't much, but it was something, a secret alliance forming under the radar, piecing together clues one by one.

The mystery was far from solved, but for the first time, Jack felt like they were closing in on the truth. And whoever the Gladiator Thief was, they were running out of shadows to hide in.

CHAPTER 7: THE CLOSE CALL

Jack sat cross-legged in his dorm, squinting at the call sheet. The pages blurred together in a swirl of highlighted chaos. "Why do they make these in a font smaller than oxygen molecules?"

Mia leaned over his shoulder, smiling. "You're holding it upside down."

"Oh. Right." He flipped it, face burning. "That explains the chaos."

"You could've just asked me to read it," she said gently. "You know I don't mind."

Jack exhaled, rubbing the back of his neck. "Yeah, but that's not exactly the heroic image I'm going for. 'Detective of Mill Bay: can't read his own script.'"

"You're not supposed to read it," Mia said with a smirk. "You're supposed to live it."

Jack looked up, and their eyes met for a beat longer than either expected. "That's... surprisingly inspiring," he said. "You should put that on a T-shirt."

"Only if I can put your face on it too."

"Then it'll never sell."

They both laughed, the sound soft and easy—a rare calm before the chaos to come.

Jack joined the *Gladiator Academy* crew on set for a major filming day. Today's schedule: a pivotal battle sequence. Jack's Retiarius, towering, net-wielding, all presence and reach, was set to shine. But his head wasn't fully in it. The profiles he and Mia had combed through last night still nagged at him: gaps in résumés, red flags, and the shadow of the Gladiator Thief.

The Myrmidons took their marks, armor flashing in the sun as they moved like a single body—precise, relentless. Anthony's grin was unmistakable even behind the discipline; he was born for spectacle. Jack smiled despite himself, then stepped onto his own platform for the overhead shot.

"Action!"

He flowed through the choreography: wide trident arcs, light-footed pivots, the net a ghost at his hip. Then an ugly creak. The platform shifted. The wood bowed under his heel.

Jack launched backward on instinct. A board split where his weight had been. Gasps burst around the set.

"Cut! Hold!" Trainers swarmed the platform.

Heart pounding, Jack scanned the ring of faces. The

Myrmidons stood in a cluster, helmets down. One tilted his head, subtle, almost curious. Or satisfied.

Mia appeared at his side, pale. "Are you okay?"

"Fine," he said, voice tight. He stared at the split timber. "That wasn't an accident."

"What do you mean?"

"That board was loosened. And they knew I'd be here."

Mia's eyes widened. "You think you're a target?"

Jack swallowed. Marcus Trent's growl from earlier "You know what to do" rattled through his skull. If Marcus was calling shots, someone inside had to be carrying them out.

Filming resumed, but the arena no longer felt like a stage; it felt like a snare. Jack couldn't identify the Myrmidon with the tilted head because they blended in so well with each other. He saw Anthony step forward to help and get pulled back by the group.

That night in the dorms, Jack and Mia spread notes across his bunk.

"If they're trying to scare you off, they're getting desperate," Mia said, pacing. "That's... good? In a way?"

"Or reckless," Jack said. "If I'd been half a beat slower..."

He cut himself off and pulled the Myrmidon files

back up. They zeroed in on three with records. One name stuck: Broderick Johnson. A bar fight in Mill Bay years ago, near Skeleton Cove. He left town, then reappeared on the Uprising crew. The words assault charge and theft jumped off the page. "If this is right," he said quietly, "Broderick Johnson has to be our number one suspect. A criminal past, the same moves as the thief, and access to all the props? He could have setup the accident today as well. It lines up too perfectly."

Mia frowned, tapping the screen. "Maybe too perfectly. But until we find someone else who fits, he's at the top of our list and we find out where he's been."

"Jack… if they sabotaged a platform, what's next?"

"Whatever it is," he said, steady now, "they underestimated me today. They won't again."

He lay awake later, listening to Anthony's easy breathing. Armor alike, movements alike, eyes behind helmets. The arena wasn't just make-believe. It was a battlefield. And he was done playing defense.

CHAPTER 8: THE CHASE IN THE LOT

The studio lot slept under a wash of moonlight. Crickets. Leaves. Silence.

Jack couldn't. The platform, the tilted helmet, the sense of being watched, loop, loop, loop.

1:43 a.m.

A shadow crossed the slice of light under the door.

Jack froze. Then he was moving, hoodie, sneakers, a hand on Anthony's shoulder.

"What?" Anthony mumbled.

"Someone's out there. I'm following."

Anthony was instantly awake. "Give me ten seconds."

They slipped into the night. The figure cut through the lot toward the props building. Jack and Anthony ducked behind stacked crates, breath held.

"What are they doing?" Anthony whispered.

"Let's find out."

The door eased shut behind the figure. Jack pressed to the window, peering through dusty glass. Inside, a narrow flashlight beam slid along shelves. It flashed off something gold, the curve of a gladiator helmet.

"It's one of them," Jack murmured.

"The Thief?" Anthony breathed.

The light skated to the production office safe. The figure worked the dial like a routine. Click. Open. A hand darted in, then a small bag vanished over a shoulder.

The door creaked. Jack and Anthony flattened against the wall as the figure stepped out and moved quickly into the shadows.

They followed. Silent. Focused. Then Jack's toe nicked a loose rock, it skittered across asphalt with a traitor's clatter.

The figure froze.

"Run," Jack hissed.

They bolted. Between sound stages, down narrow alleys, across empty bays. The thief vaulted crates; Jack's court footwork kept him close. Anthony scrambled, nearly toppling, then righted.

The chase burst into the backlot, past Roman columns and painted facades. A security light framed the thief's silhouette for a heartbeat, the gleam of a gladiator helmet.

Then they were sprinting for the perimeter fence. The thief climbed like a cat and disappeared beyond the razor line of horizon.

Anthony doubled over, panting. "Gone."

"Not for long," Jack said, scanning the darkness.

Back in the dorm, adrenaline still sparking, they called Mia. She slipped inside minutes later, hair mussed, eyes sharp.

"You look like you sprinted the entire lot," she said. "What happened?"

Jack laid it out. The safe. The bag.

"They didn't take a helmet," Mia said, already on her tablet. "They took the gold necklace, the real one from Rise of the Empire. It's locked up because it's worth a fortune." She tapped again. "And it has a GPS tracker in the clasp."

Jack leaned in. "Can we trace it?"

"I am." A map popped up, one blinking dot. Lot perimeter. "It hasn't moved since early this morning. If they still have it, we can follow the signal." She bit her lip. "But the studio won't call the police on 'missing props and accidents.' We're on our own."

Anthony grinned despite himself. "So, we catch them and get the credit."

"Or we get hurt," Jack said. "They outran us tonight

and opened a safe like it was a paper bag."

Mia nodded. "Then we plan this like a scene, not a chase. I'll monitor the tracker and update you. You two follow the signal. If anything feels wrong, we pull back."

"Agreed," Jack said. "No solo heroics."

They bent over the map. The dot pulsed back at them.

Following the blinking GPS signal, Jack and Anthony traced the necklace's last known location to a stretch of dirt road just inside the studio's perimeter fence. The night air was heavy with fog, muffling their footsteps as they searched the area with their flashlights.

"It should be right here," Anthony said, glancing at the tablet. "But the signal just stopped."

Jack crouched, brushing aside a patch of gravel. Something small fluttered in the beam of his light — a folded scrap of paper weighed down by a rock. He picked it up and unfolded it, the handwriting jagged and hurried.

GIVE UP AND STOP.

They exchanged uneasy looks.

"So much for subtle," Anthony muttered.

Jack's jaw tightened. "They know we're close. And until we figure out who's behind this we can't trust anyone."

"We loop in Anna and Bennett," Jack added. "Not just drive-bys, real digging. If the thief ties back to Marcus, they can watch his 'academy' without raising suspicion."

Anthony nodded. "Practice fields are already nearby."

Jack called Anna. She answered, groggy but listening.

"The Thief stole a real gold necklace," he said. "It's tagged. We'll try to track the signal. Can you and Bennett keep eyes on Marcus and try to get inside his place for a closer look?"

"We've got practice near there tomorrow," Anna said. "We'll swing by the Tiki Club after for updates."

When he hung up, Mia eyed the map again, frowning. "One thing bothers me. Why a necklace? Up to now they've stolen tools, armor, helmets, gear that supports the stunt-robbery pattern."

Jack folded his arms. "Exactly. A necklace doesn't help rob a bank."

"Maybe they're just cashing out," Anthony offered.

"It doesn't fit," Jack said. "Feels like misdirection, something flashy to make us chase the wrong thread while they prep their real move."

Silence pulled tight for a beat.

Mia's voice was quiet. "If they're that calculating... we're not chasing a thrill seeker. We're chasing a planner."

"Then we plan better," Jack said. "Mia, are you ok to watch the GPS to see if it comes back?"

Mia nodded and they started packing up for the night.

As Mia packed up her tablet and the others headed back toward bed, Mia paused, glancing out across the dim studio lot. The necklace was gone; the thief had vanished into the night—and one more thing didn't add up.

"Darius wasn't here tonight," Mia said quietly.

Anthony turned. "What do you mean?"

"When the theft happened," Mia replied, her voice tightening. "He was supposed to be filming a late-night promo with the crew. But nobody saw him. Not once."

Mia met Jack's gaze, understanding dawning in his eyes. "So, while we were chasing the thief…"

Mia nodded. "Darius Slate was missing."

CHAPTER 9: SMOKE AND MIRRORS

The Tiki Club's cozy hum did nothing for the knot in their stomachs. Jack, Mia, Anthony, Anna, and Bennett huddled at a corner table, voices low. Grilled fish and lake breeze drifted through the room; nobody touched their plates.

"We have to say it out loud," Mia murmured. "Darius Slate. If he disappears every time there's a robbery, we can't rule him out."

Silence fell. Anthony's fork clinked against his plate. "You're kidding," he said, jaw tight. "Darius is Myron. He's not some thief."

Jack stared at his napkin, where timelines and arrows webbed together. "I don't want it to be him either," he said. "But patterns matter. He's never around when a heist hits. He has access, training, resources. If it's not him, why does the trail keep pointing his way?"

"He's a star," Anthony shot back. "He doesn't need

money. What's the motive?"

"Thrill. Control," Mia said quietly. "We don't know. We just know the windows line up."

Anna folded her arms. "And if it isn't Darius, we still have Marcus Trent and Broderick Johnson. Marcus keeps slipping us, Broderick's got a record... but every time we close in, the trail fogs."

Bennett nodded. "Especially since we lost the GPS signal."

Jack's head snapped up. "What?"

"The necklace," Mia said. "The tracker went dark. I checked at sunrise. It's gone."

A cold drop hit Jack's spine. "They knew we were following it."

"Either they disabled the clasp or ditched it," Mia said. "Either way, bye-bye breadcrumb."

Anthony rubbed his temples. "So, we're back to zero."

"Not zero," Jack said, though frustration bled through. "We still have our three: Marcus, Broderick, and yeah Darius."

Anthony stared at the table. "How do we even investigate Darius? He's wrapped in handlers and security. He breathes on a schedule."

"Then we learn the schedule," Jack said. "If he's clean, we'll prove it. If he's not..."

Mia leaned in. "We need eyes, timestamps, and

something physical, video, props, anything that ties a suspect to a heist window."

Anna and Bennett exchanged a look. "We'll keep at Marcus," Anna said. "But it's like he feels us watching."

"Maybe he does," Jack said. "Or he has someone tipping him off. Either way, we adapt."

Anthony crossed his arms. "It feels impossible. The tracker's dead, Darius might be involved, Marcus is a ghost... it's like trying to grab smoke."

"Smoke and mirrors," Jack said. "Which means someone's staging distractions. If they're working this hard to misdirect us, they're worried."

Mia's eyes flicked around the table. "So: plan?"

Jack exhaled and started assigning: "Anna, Bennett, shadow Marcus. No heroics. Log everything, times, visitors, plates, bikes. If he runs drills with anyone, record faces."

Anna nodded. "We'll rotate between practice and stakeouts."

"Mia," Jack continued, "scrub Darius's calendar. Cross-check his 'meetings' with robbery windows. Who signs him out? Who drives? I want names."

"I can pull call sheets, shuttle logs, and door swipes," she said. "If his alibis are fake, the paperwork won't match."

"Anthony and I take Broderick," Jack finished.

"Where he goes after training, who he texts, whether he's got access to gear off-hours. We keep it quiet and we keep it boring."

Anthony swallowed, then nodded. "Fine. But if we're wrong about Darius…"

"Then we clear him," Jack said. "We follow the truth, not the headline."

Uneasy looks circled the table, settling into resolve. For the first time, the scope of it pressed down on Jack, the size of the machine they were poking, the talent of the person hiding inside it.

Somewhere between set calls and security gates, the real face of the Gladiator Thief waited. They just had to cut through the smoke before the next heist—and before the mirrors turned back on them.

CHAPTER 10: THE STAR'S SHADOW

The rec room at the studio dorms were deserted except for the hum of the vending machine and the neon glow of an old arcade cabinet. Jack wiped the sweat off his palms and squinted at the screen. "You're cheating."

"I'm winning," Mia corrected, mashing buttons as her gladiator avatar spun into a flawless combo. "Maybe if you blocked once in a while—"

"Detectives don't block, we anticipate."

"You anticipated my victory then."

Jack groaned as his character crumpled in defeat. "Best of three?"

"You said that two rounds ago."

"Yeah, but this time I mean it."

"You always mean it."

She leaned against the machine, her laughter bubbling over as Jack inserted another coin with exaggerated determination. "Fine," she said. "If you win this round, I'll let you pick dinner."

Jack grinned. "And if you win?"

"You owe me a milkshake from the Tiki Club."

"You're on."

Ten minutes later, Jack was sliding a chocolate milkshake across the counter with mock defeat. "Remind me never to underestimate your button-mashing skills again."

Mia smirked. "Remind me never to underestimate your ability to keep losing with style."

Jack raised his glass in a toast. "To losing with style."

She clinked hers against his. "And to catching thieves who can't hide forever."

Jack had spent the rest of the week pushing himself to the limit at *Gladiator Academy*, hours of filming small scenes showing his characters trident moves and precision net work. To keep fresh, he had punishing sparring sessions that left his muscles aching but his instincts razor-sharp. Yet even as his body adapted to the rhythm of filming, his mind refused to rest.

The thought had been circling him for days, unshakable:
Darius Slate was too perfect. Too smooth. Too controlled.

Jack had begun watching the rising star the way a detective studies a suspect, or a player studies a rival before a championship game. On-screen, Darius was everything the *Gladiator Uprising* franchise needed:

the reluctant hero turned warrior, magnetic, flawless, every line delivered with effortless conviction. But off-camera, Jack was beginning to notice the cracks beneath the polish.

It started small. Darius vanished right before key Myrmidon filming sessions, returning minutes before cameras rolled, sweaty, winded, but collected. He refused to let anyone handle his gear, insisting he maintain it himself. And the way he chased danger, it wasn't performance. It was appetite.

Jack saw it firsthand during the filming of a major arena fight. Darius ignored cues, charging into stunts early, striking harder than rehearsed. He demanded "authenticity," urging the Myrmidons to hit like they meant it. The director's jaw tightened, but Darius only smiled.
It wasn't acting. It was something darker a need to feel control in chaos.

Later that evening, Jack lingered behind the barracks, half in shadow. Darius stood a few yards away, speaking in low tones with Broderick Johnson. Broderick's name was already underlined in red in Jack and Mia's notes: minor theft, bar fights, short temper.

Jack couldn't hear the words, but he saw Darius lean in close, eyes sharp, expression unreadable. Broderick nodded, glanced over his shoulder, then slipped off into the dark.

Jack waited a beat, then stepped forward.

"You seem busy for a guy with a packed filming schedule," he said.

Darius turned, his signature grin already in place. "Gotta stay sharp, Sawyer. This role takes more than good lighting."

"Seems like you're spending a lot of time with the Myrmidons off camera," Jack said evenly.

Darius brushed a hand through his hair, the picture of charm. "Something like that. Myron's a leader. I need to understand how my men think, move, breathe. Makes the fights more believable."

Jack didn't blink. He'd seen this before, the polished deflection, the conversational sleight of hand. Darius was answering everything and saying nothing.

"And Broderick?" Jack asked. "How does he fit into your character study?"

For a fraction of a second, Darius's smile thinned. A flicker of calculation passed behind his eyes. "Broderick's got experience. He's helping me with a few... extracurriculars."

"Extracurriculars like what?" Jack pressed.

Darius's smirk returned, practiced and cool. "Wouldn't you like to know?" He clapped Jack on the shoulder, friendly on the surface, firm enough to sting. "Get some rest, Sawyer. Big scene tomorrow."

Jack watched him stride off toward his trailer, cape flicking behind him in the evening wind. His unease solidified into certainty.

Darius Slate was hiding something.

Jack lingered in the shadows after Darius walked off, his instincts prickling. Broderick had glanced around nervously, then slipped toward the far end of the lot, moving faster than someone with nothing to hide.

Hoping to catch up with him Jack took off at a sprint as soon as he heard the click of Darius's trailer door.

Broderick cut through the maze of sound stages and prop buildings, his stride deliberate. Jack kept his distance, staying low behind a stack of crates. When Broderick reached the motorcycle garage, he paused, looking both ways before unlocking the door. The metallic click echoed in the night air.

Jack watched as Broderick wheeled out a black motorcycle—sleek, fast, identical to the ones the Myrmidons used during training. He revved the engine once, then stuffed something into his jacket pocket before speeding off into the darkness.

By the time Jack reached the garage, the smell of gasoline still hung in the air. On the workbench, a half-burned piece of paper caught his attention. He pulled it closer under the light—part of a map, with the words bank route and Mill Bay barely visible.

Jack's pulse quickened. Broderick was hiding something and he wasn't working alone.

Later that night, when Jack told Mia and Anthony

what he saw, neither seemed convinced.

"You think Darius Slate is involved because Broderick took a late-night joyride?" Anthony said, shaking his head. "Come on, Jack. You're seeing patterns that aren't there."

Mia folded her arms. "You've been pushing this theory for days. Darius is a control freak, sure, but that doesn't make him a criminal."

Jack stared out the dorm window, his jaw tight. "Maybe not. But Broderick's working for someone. And if it's not Darius... then who else has that kind of pull?"

No one answered. But Jack couldn't shake the image of Darius's calm, confident smile—and the way it never quite reached his eyes.

Later that night, Jack found Mia in the props room, her face lit by the glow of her tablet as she scrolled through inventory logs.

"We need to focus on Darius," Jack said quietly.

Mia looked up, frowning. "Darius? You really think he's behind the heists?"

"He disappears right before the robberies," Jack said. "I saw him talking to Broderick tonight. The timing, the secrecy, it's all too clean. We have to track where he goes when he's not on set."

Mia hesitated, then pulled up his schedule. "He's marked as being in 'meetings' during almost every major heist," she said slowly. "But there's no proof those meetings actually happen."

Jack's jaw tightened. "Then we'll make proof. If he's acting off-screen too, we'll find out who he really is when the spotlight's off."

Jack didn't sleep that night. Darius's smug grin and Broderick's night ride looped in his mind like a film reel stuck on repeat.

Just as dawn began to creep through the dorm window, his phone buzzed violently on the nightstand. Groggy, he grabbed it—and froze.

Breaking News: Another Gladiator-Style Robbery in Mill Bay.

The photo attached to the alert showed the same distinctive armor, the same sleek motorcycle tearing through the parking lot of a jewelry exchange. It was nearly identical to the footage from the earlier heists, down to the symbols painted on the thief's chest plate.

Anthony stirred on the bunk below. "Jack? What's going on?"

"Another one," Jack said quietly. "Last night."

Within the hour, the Academy buzzed with whispers. Crew members huddled around phones and tablets, replaying the footage on loop. But one fact stood out to everyone, Darius Slate had been on set the entire time. Dozens of people had seen him rehearsing a live stunt sequence until midnight. There was no way he could've been the one in the armor.

"So, it wasn't him," Mia said later that morning as they reviewed the news footage together. "He's got an airtight alibi."

Jack stared at the blurry figure on the screen, the thief vaulting over a counter with the same effortless grace he'd seen Darius use in combat drills. "Maybe. Or maybe someone wants it to look that way."

Anthony frowned. "Jack, you've got to admit, it doesn't add up. Darius was surrounded by people all night."

Jack didn't respond. The gears in his head were already turning. Every heist, every move, every piece of armor—it was all too deliberate. Someone was pulling strings, and Darius might not have been the hand behind the mask… but he still felt like part of the illusion.

As the day wore on, Jack watched Darius on set, laughing with the crew, the picture of innocence. Yet something in his eyes—sharp, distant, calculating— kept Jack's suspicions alive.

The Gladiator Thief had struck again, but this time, the performance was perfect. Too perfect.

And Jack couldn't shake the feeling that Darius Slate was still playing a role.

CHAPTER 11:
INTO THE VAULT

The sun dipped low over the studio lot, casting long shadows across the training grounds. The day had dragged on, filled with tension and unanswered questions. The robbery had left everyone uneasy, but the official word from the production team was simple: "It's a coincidence."

Jack didn't believe in coincidences. Not anymore.

He sat on the edge of his bunk, tapping a pencil against his notebook where he'd been sketching timelines and suspect names. Darius Slate. Marcus Trent. Broderick Johnson. Every path led back to them, but Darius's name was the one that refused to fade.

"You're really still on this?" Anthony asked, leaning against the doorframe. "Jack, Darius couldn't have done it. He was literally surrounded by people when the robbery happened."

Jack didn't look up. "Then why does everything about him feel staged? The timing, the attitude, the way he controls every move on set—it's all performance."

Mia sighed from across the room. "You've been running yourself into the ground. Maybe you need to step back before this turns into an obsession."

Jack met her gaze, calm but resolute. "That's exactly what he wants—to make me second-guess what I'm seeing. If I'm wrong, I'll admit it. But if I'm right…"

"You'll do what?" Anthony interrupted.

Jack stood, slipping on his jacket and tucking his notebook into his pocket. "I'll prove it. I'm going to his trailer tonight."

Anthony's eyes widened. "You can't be serious. If you get caught—"

"Then I'll say I got lost looking for the props department," Jack said, flashing a faint grin that didn't reach his eyes.

Mia shook her head. "Jack, this is a bad idea."

"Maybe," Jack replied, opening the door. "But it's the only one that feels right."

As he stepped into the cool night air, the sounds of the studio faded behind him. He didn't know what he would find in Darius's trailer—but for the first time, he felt like he was finally chasing something real.

Jack Sawyer moved silently through the moonlit expanse of the studio lot, his heart pounding as he approached Darius Slate's trailer. The luxury rig stood apart from the others, sleek, silver, and spotless, a sharp contrast to the weathered prop shacks of *Gladiator Academy*.

If Darius was connected to the Gladiator Thief, the truth had to be hidden in there.

Jack crouched near the back entrance, scanning the lot. The world was still: just the hum of a distant generator and the soft hiss of wind through the fake colosseum arches. Anthony had begged to come, but Jack had refused. Fewer people meant fewer chances to get caught.

He took a slow breath, pulled a set of slender tools from his pocket, borrowed from the props department, and slid them into the lock. A gentle twist, a soft click. The door eased open. Jack slipped inside and shut it quietly behind him.

The air inside was warm, faintly scented with cologne and coffee. Polished marble counters gleamed under low amber lights. Designer suits hung beside racks of Myrmidon armor. Every surface screamed star power.

Jack ignored it. He wasn't here to admire Darius Slate's success; he was here to expose it.

He moved methodically: desk drawers, cabinets, the space behind framed photos of Darius with co-stars and producers. Nothing. Then, as he turned toward the back, he noticed a smaller door half-hidden behind the wardrobe.

He knelt, testing the handle. Locked.

His pulse quickened. This is it.

Using the same tools, he jimmied the latch until it gave. Inside sat a duffel bag, stuffed tight. He dragged it out, unzipped it and froze.

Inside were modified gladiator props: reinforced swords, armour with secret compartments and plated thicker than the standard stunt gear. Beneath them lay blueprints of multiple banks, each annotated with notes, security blind spots, guard rotations, escape routes. And at the very bottom: stacks of cash, neatly banded.

Jack's breath hitched. This is the smoking gun.

Then—rattle.
The front latch.

Jack's blood went cold. He ducked behind the leather sofa just as the door swung open.

Darius Slate stepped inside, backlit by the studio lights. He paused, scanning the room with a predator's stillness. His eyes flicked toward the back, and for a heartbeat, Jack thought he'd been caught. But Darius only exhaled sharply and reached for his phone.

"Marcus," he said, voice taut. "It's me. I'm not keeping this duffel bag in my trailer anymore. You want it hidden; you deal with it yourself."

Jack's stomach dropped. Marcus. Marcus Trent.

So, Darius wasn't the puppet master he was the puppet.

"I'm not your errand boy," Darius muttered as he hung up, tossing the phone onto the counter. He turned toward the back.

Jack moved. Swift, silent. He snatched the duffel, slipped past the kitchen counter, and darted for the exit.

The night air hit him like a slap, cool and sharp. He sprinted across the lot, the bag thudding against his side. Every step echoed with questions: Was Darius working for Marcus or being framed by him? Either way, the game was much bigger than he'd realized.

He didn't stop running until the dorms came into view. Bursting through the door, he startled Anthony awake.

"Jack?" Anthony blinked, bleary. "What happened?"

Jack dropped the duffel onto the floor with a heavy thud. "We've got proof," he said, catching his breath. "Darius Slate's tied to the Gladiator Thief."

Anthony stared at the bag, wide-eyed.

You're sure this was in Darius's trailer?" Mia asked, her voice barely above a whisper.

"Positive," Jack said, unzipping the duffel again. "It was hidden behind a locked compartment. Look at this—blueprints, cash, even reinforced prop weapons."

Anthony whistled low. "That's… a lot more than method acting."

Mia dug through the papers, her eyes catching on a small flash drive tucked between two stacks of notes. "Hold on—what's this?"

They loaded the drive onto her tablet. Grainy security footage flickered to life: Marcus Trent and Broderick Johnson in what looked like a storage room, surrounded by prop armor. The sound was muted, but Marcus's gestures were unmistakable, pointing at the helmets, at a map on the wall, and then toward a duffel bag identical to the one sitting on Jack's bunk.

"That's them," Jack said, leaning forward. "Marcus and Broderick. Planning something. This is exactly what we need."

Mia hesitated. "Then we take it to the police."

Jack frowned. "And tell them what? That we broke into Darius Slate's trailer?"

"We'll figure that out later," she said firmly. "If this ties Marcus and Broderick to the robberies, it's worth the risk."

An hour later, Mia stood in the small Mill Bay police substation, her tablet on the desk between two detectives. Jack and Anthony waited outside, watching through the glass as she spoke, her tone calm but insistent.

When she finally stepped out, her expression was

grim.

"They don't believe it," she said flatly. "They said the footage could've come from anywhere—that it's too grainy to prove when or where it was taken. And since the blueprints and money don't have serial numbers, they're calling it 'circumstantial at best.'"

"What about the trailer?" Jack asked.

"They said Darius reported a break-in last night," Mia replied, her frustration bubbling over. "They're more interested in finding out who 'stole his personal property' than checking what was inside it."

Anthony groaned. "So, we're the suspects now?"

"Not officially," Mia said, "but they hinted that if we 'stumble across any more evidence,' we should turn it in immediately. They think we're meddling."

Jack stared at the duffel bag on the table, its contents spread out like puzzle pieces no one wanted to solve. "This was supposed to be our lead," he muttered. "Now it's just making everything worse."

Mia crossed her arms, her voice steady but edged with frustration. "If Darius really is behind this, he's covering his tracks faster than we can expose them. The police won't move unless they have something solid—and we just handed them a bag that makes us look guilty."

Jack's jaw tightened. "Then we'll find proof they can't ignore. We've come too far to give up now."

He glanced toward the window, where the reflection of the duffel's dark fabric glimmered in the glass like a shadow—evidence that once looked like salvation, now threatening to pull them all under.

CHAPTER 12:
FIGHT OR FLEE

Jack's heart still pounded from his narrow escape the night before. He had barely managed to slip away with the duffel bag, but Darius Slate was no fool, he'd already turned the situation to his advantage.

The sun had barely risen, but Jack was already back in the dorm, pacing while the others sat in uneasy silence. Mia scrolled through her tablet, scanning news updates, while Anthony stared out the window toward the training lot.

"You're not going to like this," Mia said, her voice tight. "Darius reported the break-in to the press this morning. He's playing it up for them, calling it 'a cowardly act by someone jealous of his success.'"

Anthony turned, grimacing. "And the cops are buying it?"

"Completely," Mia said. "Security's doubled, and they've started questioning crew members. Everyone's talking about 'the trailer thief.' He's acting like he's the victim."

Jack stopped pacing. "He's enjoying this."

"More than enjoying it," Anthony said. "I saw him this morning near the set. He was all smiles, telling people he's sure the police will 'find whoever's responsible.'"

Jack's jaw tightened. "He's taunting us."

"He knows exactly what he's doing," Mia added. "The duffel bag was supposed to be our proof, and now it's making us look like criminals. The police said the evidence could've come from anywhere."

Jack sat down on the edge of his bunk, rubbing his temples. "He's flipped the whole thing on us. We found the truth, and somehow, we're the ones under suspicion."

"So, what now?" Anthony asked quietly. "If we push harder, we'll just look guiltier."

Jack looked up, his expression hardening. "Then we stop reacting and start fighting back. If Darius thinks he can hide behind his fame and charm, he's wrong. We're going to prove it, and we'll do it on our terms."

The group exchanged uneasy glances. The police might have dismissed them, the studio might have believed Darius, but Jack's resolve had only deepened.

The duffel bag that once seemed like their biggest lead was now their biggest problem, and it had just made the most powerful man on set their enemy.

A knock at the door cut the room silent. Jack

motioned for everyone to stay put and cracked the door open. Darius Slate leaned in, the polished charm that filled magazine covers folded into a dangerous calm.

"Morning, Sawyer," Darius said. His smile was casual but cold. "You and I need to talk."

Jack stepped outside, closing the door. Darius chuckled, folding his arms. "Kid, you've got guts. But you're playing in a league way above your head. You don't know what you've stepped into."

Jack met him without flinching. "I know enough. You're not a hero, Darius. You're helping a criminal."

Darius's smile thinned. "Dangerous to say that without proof."

"Oh, I've got proof," Jack said, louder than he'd intended. "Blueprints, marked escape routes, cash. Everything. It's gone to the police."

"The same police that are looking for a trailer burglar?" said Daruis.

Jack stayed silent.

Darius stepped closer, close enough that Jack could smell the coffee on his breath. "Listen," he said, low. "You walk away from this, and nothing happens to you or your friends. Keep pushing and accidents happen. I know you were in my trailer last night."

Jack felt the warning like cold water. Darius leaned in, voice barely a whisper. "You're supposed to be my rival on screen. Don't make me cut your role short.

Permanently."

Jack's jaw clenched. "I don't scare that easy."

Darius let out a short, controlled laugh. "Good. Then let's put that to the test." He turned and walked away, leaving the threat hanging between them.

Jack shut the door, locked it, and walked back into the room where his friends sat frozen. "He knows we have the evidence," Jack said. "And he's protecting Marcus Trent."

Mia's eyes hardened. "Then we take this somewhere he can't control the story. We make it public, media, social feeds, independent reporters. Pull both of them into the light."

Anthony swallowed and nodded, no bravado left. "And fast. If he's willing to threaten us, we don't get a second shot."

Jack looked around at the faces he trusted, Mia's steady calm, Anna's fierce concentration, Bennett's earnest worry, Anthony's shaky courage. They were in this together. There was no turning back.

"Okay," Jack said, voice steady. "We expose them. We do it smart, and we do it now. Fight or flee there's only one choice."

They leaned in, drawing up a plan that would force a showdown: cameras, timestamps, witnesses, and a public place where neither Darius nor Marcus could pull the strings. The gamble felt enormous, but so did the stakes.

Outside, somewhere between the polished trailers and the fake stone arches, a real danger was circling. Inside the tiny office, a handful of teenagers prepared to meet it head-on.

CHAPTER 13: THE ADRENALINE JUNKIE

Jack sat on the edge of his bunk, gripping the empty duffel bag as Darius Slate's threat replayed in his head. Darius wasn't robbing banks for money; he was doing it for the rush, and he was able to get Marcus and Broderick to fill in when needed. Jack's instincts said that Daruis was behind everything even though the evidence didn't show that yet. He was sure that Darius loved the high of outsmarting everyone. The game itself was the reward.

Jack exhaled, his mind racing. He'd read about people like Darius before, adrenaline junkies who needed danger the way others needed air. They always thought they were invincible, until the crash came. The only question was whether Darius would burn out before someone else got hurt.

Mia sat beside him, scrolling through articles on her tablet. "He's built different," she murmured. "No money problems. No reason to risk anything. He's been famous since seventeen, but it's not enough. He needs the danger."

Jack nodded. "The armor, the theatrics, the heists, it's all one big performance. He's not stealing. He's acting."

Anthony, pacing near the window, looked pale. "It's a stretch. Not every heist lines up with his filming schedule. He vanishes sometimes, a robbery happens, and then he comes back like he's running on pure adrenaline but sometimes he's here the whole time."

Jack clenched his jaw. "Then we need to figure this out before someone else pays the price."

The door opened and Anna and Bennett slipped in, fresh from their latest stakeout of Marcus Trent. "We've got a problem," Anna said quietly. "Trent's meeting someone late at night. And this time, we saw who."

Jack stood. "Who?"

Bennett hesitated. "Broderick Johnson."

A chill ran through the room. Broderick, the Myrmidon with a record. The one Darius had been mentoring. If he was meeting Trent, the operation wasn't just some side hustle. It was a network.

"They're planning something," Mia said. "If Broderick's the bridge between Marcus and Darius, this goes way beyond one man."

Jack's mind was already turning. "Then we hit them

where it hurts. Somewhere they can't spin or silence the truth."

Anthony scoffed. "Good luck. Darius owns the headlines, and the studio will protect their golden boy no matter what."

Jack's eyes sharpened. "Then we go public our way."

Mia's lips curved into a grin. "Social media."

"Exactly," Jack said. "If we leak the footage and evidence online, it'll spread faster than they can bury it."

Anthony frowned. "And when Darius finds out? He'll come after us."

Jack met his gaze. "Then we make sure he doesn't get the chance."

They worked for hours, piecing together their plan. Mia compiled footage, timestamps, and proof linking Darius, Marcus, and Broderick. Anna and Bennett tracked Myrmidon movements. Anthony watched for unusual activity on the lot.

Finally, Jack broke the silence. "We need Naomi."

Anthony's eyebrows shot up. "Naomi Tanaka? From Maui?"

Jack nodded. His old partner-in-detective-work turned investigative journalist had a knack for uncovering the truth and a following big enough to make it stick. "If anyone can blow this open, it's her."

He dialed her number. After a few rings, Naomi's

familiar voice came through, calm and amused. "Jack Sawyer. I was wondering when you'd drag me into another mystery."

Jack smiled despite himself. "You busy?"

"Always," she said, "but something tells me this one's worth it."

He gave her the rundown, and by the time he finished, Naomi was all in. "Send me everything," she said. "I'll have it live before they even know what's happening."

Jack ended the call and turned to his team. "This is it. We go live tonight. We'll frame it so Darius looks like Marcus's pawn. If it's true, great. If it's not, it might force him to show his hand."

By sunset, they regrouped at the Tiki Club, their safest base. At exactly 8:00 p.m., Naomi's exposé hit the internet: The Gladiator Thief: Hollywood's Golden Boy controlled by a nobody. It included everything footage, photos, blueprints, and the names connecting Darius, Marcus, and Broderick.

The internet exploded.

The fallout from Naomi's article hit like a lightning strike. Within hours, the story was everywhere, every headline, every trending feed, every entertainment show dissecting every word.

The team decided to split up. Jack, Anthony, and Mia would try and keep eyes Darius and Anna and Bennett would try to follow Marcus. They had no idea where Broderick would turn up so hoped for the best.

For Marcus Trent and Broderick Johnson, it meant the end. The studio had cut all ties, their names were trending for all the wrong reasons, and any chance of salvaging their reputations had vanished overnight.

Jack, Anthony, and Mia setup at a table by a window in one of the production offices that faced Darius' trailer. He had clearly seen the news on his phone and stormed inside slamming the door. A couple hours later he emerged with a dark expression on his face and headed towards the motorcycle garage.

Jack saw Broderick heading in that direction as well. "Let's split up. You two follow Daruis and I'll try to keep up with Broderick." He spoke. He quickly ran out and followed Broderick as he moved towards the open loading bay. He saw Anthony and Mia at the far end of the building going through a side door.

Jack hid behind some shelving and crates with a view of Broderick tuning his motorcycle. The stuntman barely glanced up when Darius approached, his expression a mix of guilt and defiance.

"Rough day," Darius said casually. "Press isn't exactly on your side."

Broderick grunted. Darius gave an easy smile. "Maybe. But if you're smart, you'll keep your head down. Lay low. The police are looking for scapegoats."

"Like me?" Broderick asked bitterly.

"You said it, not me." Jack could see something glinting in Darius' hand. As Broderick turned away, Darius reached out to clap him on the shoulder. In one smooth motion, the missing necklace slipped from his palm into the side pouch of the motorcycle. A friendly pat, a sympathetic nod, and a trap was set.

"Stay out of trouble, Broderick," Darius said, walking off. "No one's going to save you twice."

Broderick fired up his motorcycle and tore off in a cloud of tire smoke.

Jack pulled out his phone and texted Anthony and Mia. "Get the tablet! Daruis planted the necklace on Broderick." Mia sent a quick thumbs up and said meet at the dorm.

As soon as they arrived back Mia had the glowing GPS dot on the screen. Anthony looked out the window with a serious expression on his face. "Jack, as soon as we headed for the tablet Daruis disappeared."

Anna and Benett were setup in the field near Marcus's house and heard the roar of an approaching motorcycle. Jack had given them a heads up that Broderick was headed that way and they got in a position to try and hear any conversation from the house.

That evening, in Marcus Trent's dimly lit garage, the

air buzzed with the sound of an idling motorcycle and desperation.

"They made us the villains," Broderick spat, pacing through piles of rusted tools and stolen props. "Darius hung us out to dry."

Marcus, leaning against the workbench, gave a low, bitter laugh. "That's what stars do, shine bright and burn everyone else."

"So, what now?" Broderick demanded. "We're broke. Blacklisted. Done."

Marcus's eyes gleamed in the flickering light. "Then we go out our own way. One last score, a jewelry store on the east side of Mill Bay. No guards, just cameras. We'll be ghosts before they even notice."

Broderick hesitated, then nodded grimly. "Fine. One last job."

An hour later, at the Tiki Club, Jack, Mia, and the others gathered around a laptop, trying to piece together the next move. The buzz of conversation faded when Mia's tablet pinged sharply.

The GPS map flashed red, a moving dot racing across the east side of town.

"It's Broderick's motorcycle," Mia breathed. "Heading toward the harbor district."

"Send it to the police!" Jack ordered.

Mia's fingers flew across the screen, forwarding the data to the authorities. Within minutes, police cruisers tore through Mill Bay, lights cutting through the night.

Marcus and Broderick thundered down the empty highway, the stolen necklace's tracker silently leading the way. They smashed through the front of the jewelry store, glass shattering like gunfire. Bags filled with diamonds. Sirens wailed.

"We've been set up!" Marcus shouted as blue and red lights flooded the street.

Broderick dropped the bag; panic etched across his face. "How—?"

Marcus didn't answer. He already knew.

Back at the Tiki Club, the tracker icon blinked to a stop. Mia exhaled. "They've been caught."

Jack nodded slowly, but something gnawed at him. "Where's Darius?"

The question hung in the air as the news feed lit up with images of the arrests. Marcus Trent and Broderick Johnson were in custody, their last job foiled before it began. But there was no sign of Darius Slate.

Jack stared at the screen. "He planned this," he said quietly.

By dawn, both were in custody—and the final threads of Darius Slate's web had begun to unravel.

The story was trending worldwide. The police were at *Gladiator Academy* with warrants. Marcus

Trent was in handcuffs on the morning news. Cameras caught him shouting, "Darius Slate's the real mastermind! I just did what he told me! That property was planted!" as officers shoved him into a squad car.

The lot was chaos, news crews swarming, crew members whispering, police cordoning off the area. Jack stood in the middle of it all his heart heavy.

Darius wasn't under anymore investigation as he had slipped past the police department's suspicion with no concrete evidence tying him to anything, but Jack knew he had a bigger part.

There was no victory, only a gnawing certainty.

Darius Slate wasn't the type to surrender.

And Jack knew deep down, this was far from over.

CHAPTER 14: THE FINAL DUEL

The revelation that Marcus Trent had orchestrated the Gladiator Thief heists sent shockwaves through Hollywood. The internet was in chaos, fans demanding answers, reporters circling the studio like vultures. But for Jack, Anthony, Mia, Anna, and Bennett, the headlines meant only one thing: the game wasn't over.

Darius Slate was still out there.

And if they'd learned anything about him, it was that he wouldn't hide forever, he'd come back for a final act.

Jack and Anthony devised a trap. With Mia and Naomi's help, they arranged a live-streamed "behind-the-scenes" broadcast from the *Gladiator Uprising* set, inviting journalists to watch an exclusive Myrmidon training session.

They knew Darius's ego wouldn't let him resist. If he was going to reclaim control of the story, he'd do it on camera, with the world watching.

The studio lights blazed like miniature suns above

the *Gladiator Academy* set, washing the arena floor in gold and shadow. Rows of cameras surrounded the perimeter, red tally lights blinking like unblinking eyes. Producers, reporters, and fans filled the stands for the highly promoted "*Gladiator Uprising*: Behind the Scenes Livestream Event."

For most people, it was a chance to see movie magic in action.

For Jack Sawyer and his friends, it was bait for a trap.

Jack adjusted the leather bracer on his arm, the trident resting against his shoulder as Anthony checked his armor beside him. Across the arena, Mia stood at a podium with a headset and a tablet to coordinate the broadcast. Her heart pounded, but she smiled for the cameras.

"Alright, everyone," she said, her voice echoing through the speakers. "We'll start with a demonstration of our combat choreography—performed by two of *Gladiator Academy*'s most promising trainees."

Applause rippled through the crowd.

Jack glanced at Anthony, who grinned nervously. "Just another day in the arena, right?"

"Yeah," Jack said, forcing a smile. "Except this time, the bad guy might actually hit back."

Mia caught his eye from across the ring and gave a subtle nod. The plan was simple: stage a mock duel to draw Darius Slate out. After Naomi's exposé and the failed jewelry store heist, Darius had vanished —but Jack knew his ego wouldn't let the story end without him in control.

Anthony twirled his prop sword. "You really think he'll show?"

Jack lifted his trident. "Oh, he'll show. He can't resist a spotlight."

The music swelled, and the demonstration began. The two clashed with choreographed precision, trident meeting sword, sand spraying with every step. Jack moved with calculated energy, his mind half in the fight, half scanning the edges of the set.

Then the audience gasped.

A shadow appeared at the top of the stairs.

Darius Slate descended like a king returning to his throne, clad in his black-and-gold Myrmidon armor. The polished metal gleamed beneath the lights, his cape trailing dramatically behind him.

"Sorry to interrupt," Darius called, his voice smooth and amplified. "But you're missing your star."

The crew froze. The camera feeds cut between confusion and awe as Darius strode into the arena.

Mia's breath caught. "Jack," she whispered into her mic. "He's here."

Jack tightened his grip on the trident. "Stay behind the podium."

Darius stepped into the ring, drawing his own blade

with theatrical grace. "How about we show them how it's really done?"

Anthony frowned. "This isn't in the script."

Darius smirked. "It is now."

Without warning, he lunged. His sword sliced through the air, the impact ringing off Jack's trident with real force. Sparks flew—literal ones, from the pyrotechnic rigs tripped by his movement.

The crowd cheered, thinking it was part of the act.

Jack stumbled back but recovered quickly. "He's fighting for real!" he shouted to Anthony.

"Then so are we!" Anthony charged forward, swinging his sword to block a second strike aimed at Jack's ribs. Darius countered effortlessly, grinning as if he were enjoying every second.

"Come on, Sawyer," he taunted. "You wanted the truth. Here it is, no cameras, no edits. Just you and me."

Jack gritted his teeth, pushing back hard. "The truth doesn't need a spotlight, Darius."

"Oh, but the world does," Darius said with a laugh, pressing forward again.

Their weapons clashed in a blur of motion. Sand sprayed. Armor cracked. The crowd's cheers turned to uneasy murmurs as the realism became too real.

Mia's voice faltered as she tried to keep the livestream sounding professional. "And... uh... what an incredible display of authenticity from our performers…"

Then she saw it.

One of the light rigs above the podium had come loose during the chaos. It dangled by a single cable, sparks sputtering near the exposed wiring.

"Jack!" she cried. "The rig!"

Darius looked up, saw the danger and smiled. "Guess we'll see who the real hero is." He shoved Jack backward and turned toward the podium.

Before Jack could react, Anthony sprinted across the arena.

"Anthony, no!" Jack shouted.

The light rig snapped free with a metallic scream. Anthony dove, tackling Mia out of the way as the heavy frame crashed to the floor where she'd been standing. The sound was deafening.

"Anthony!" Mia gasped, scrambling beside him. The crowd screamed as the broadcast cut to static.

Jack turned, fury surging through him. "That's enough!"

He charged Darius, the two colliding in a flurry of strikes that echoed through the hollow arena. Cameras flickered back online, catching the moment Jack's trident locked against Darius's sword, both straining for control.

"Lights. Camera. Deception," Darius hissed.

Darius stumbled, falling to one knee as the audience realized finally that this wasn't part of the show.

Mia helped Anthony sit up, shaken but alive. "You saved me," she whispered.

He gave a dazed grin. "Guess I just wanted a better close-up."

Darius fought like a man possessed, every move fueled by fury and pride. But Jack wasn't trying to match him in strength. He relied on instinct, fast, reactive, unpredictable. While Darius fought to perform, Jack fought to win.

Blow after blow, they circled each other, the metallic ring of weapons echoing across the set. Darius's strikes were precise, deadly, but Jack read him like a playbook, dodging, parrying, waiting for his moment.

"Marcus was the genius?" Jack taunted between strikes. "He planned every move, didn't he? Every heist, every hit, you were just the actor along for the ride!"

Darius's eyes flared red through the narrow slit of his helmet. His attacks grew faster, sloppier. Jack could see the anger consuming him.

"Careful," Jack said calmly, sidestepping another reckless swing. "You're losing your rhythm, superstar."

"Shut up!" Darius roared, his movements unravelling.

That was Jack's opening.

Darius overcommitted on a downward strike, his sword slicing empty air. Jack twisted, casting his net in one fluid motion. It wrapped around Darius's sword arm, yanking him off balance. The Myrmidon leader stumbled forward, and Jack drove the trident into the ground, its three prongs stopping inches from Darius's chest.

Darius froze, panting beneath his helmet. Then, in a surge of rage, he screamed,
"Do you think Marcus controlled me? I'm the one who planned it all! I made fools out of everyone!"

The confession echoed through the arena, straight into the live-stream cameras. Jack felt a flood of relief that he had been right to trust his instincts.

For a heartbeat, time stopped. Then chaos exploded. Crew members shouted, reporters surged forward, and security guards swarmed the set. Darius was disarmed and dragged to his knees as the world watched the fall of its golden boy in real time.

Jack stood still, chest heaving, as Darius was escorted away. He didn't need to say a word. The truth and the cameras had done the rest.

Anthony jogged up, grinning despite the tension. "Are you ok?"

Jack gave a half-smile. "Next time, let's not fight a movie star on live TV, okay?"

Anthony laughed breathlessly. "Deal."

By afternoon, the full story unraveled. Darius had started his crime spree on the first movie. Marcus Trent had figured it out almost immediately and tried blackmailing Darius, threatening to expose his role in the first heist unless he kept cooperating. Darius, desperate to protect his image, had gone along, until he was able to setup enough evidence against Marcus that Marcus was forced into helping. Marcus recruited Broderick hoping to get out from Daruis's control, but Daruis was too clever and soon had them both working for him.

Broderick Johnson had been stealing props to pay off gambling debts, which drew him into the mess. By the time he realized what he was part of, it was too late.

The Gladiator Thief saga had ended but Jack knew this wasn't just about catching criminals it was about his desire to help people and trust his instincts.

CHAPTER 15: HEROES OF MILL BAY

News of Darius Slate's arrest spread like wildfire. The revelation that the star of *Gladiator Uprising* was also the elusive Gladiator Thief sent shockwaves through Hollywood, and far beyond. Reporters swarmed the studio gates, drones hovered overhead, and police combed the set for evidence.

Jack, Anthony, Mia, Anna, and Bennett stood together, watching as Darius, Marcus Trent, and Broderick Johnson were led from the police station in handcuffs to the Jail bus, their empire of deception finally brought down.

Naomi had been recognized as the source of the initial story and Mia had ended up on camera for organizing the live stream. The cameras couldn't get enough of Mia with interviewers asking her questions to keep her talking. Her star power was clear.

Jack somehow stayed out of the spotlight; he had

been in his full armour when confronting Darius so his role in the final showdown wasn't public knowledge. The production company had decided to try and keep it a mystery to pull attention away from their stars fall from fame.

The case was closed. The truth was out. And somehow, against all odds, Jack and Anthony had helped end one of the wildest chapters in Hollywood history.

Back on set, the studio scrambled to salvage *Gladiator Uprising*'s finale. The producer's and director were on set trying to come up with a solution to end the movie when Jack suggested they change directions and get a female Gladiator to take over the franchise. He pointed at Mia and said, "she'd be perfect to take over." The director looked at Mia and spoke to the producers bringing up the news feeds from earlier. After some back and forth they came to an agreement. A climactic scene was rewritten, with Anthony stepping into Myron's place, sacrificing himself to save a new warrior played by Mia.

They had to rush the filming to the late afternoon, Jack's character's fight with Myron/Anthony would end with both characters being mortally wounded. Mia's new character would rise like a phoenix from the ashes and lead *Gladiator Uprising* in a new direction.

When the director called "cut" for the last time, Jack

couldn't help smiling.

It felt poetic.

Anthony had gone from super-fan to on-screen hero.

Mia had stepped into her own legend.

And Jack, well, he'd finally found peace with being the guy behind the scenes.

When filming wrapped, the cast and crew celebrated late into the night. But Jack and Anthony knew there was only one place they wanted to be, home.

Returning to their homes in Mill Bay felt like waking from a dream. The town had followed their adventure through every headline and livestream, and now banners hung from the lampposts downtown:

WELCOME HOME, HEROES OF MILL BAY!

The neon palm sign of the Tiki Club flickered softly in the evening haze, the sound of laughter and lake-breeze chatter spilling from the open doors. Inside, Jack sat at their usual booth the corner one scrolling through his phone while waiting for the rest of the crew.

The bell over the door jingled.

Anthony strolled in wearing a brand-new *Gladiator Uprising* T-shirt—jet-black with a neon-purple logo and, front and center, a striking image of Mia in her Myrmidon armor.

Jack nearly choked on his soda. "Oh, come on," he

said, grinning. "Really?"

Anthony spread his arms proudly. "Limited edition, baby! Straight from the studio store. They're already calling her the face of the new franchise."

Mia followed him in, rolling her eyes but smiling all the same. "I told them I wasn't doing any more promo," she said, sliding into the booth beside Jack. "But apparently, merchandising didn't get the memo."

Jack laughed. "You mean you're turning down *Gladiator Uprising* franchise? Its star was so stable."

"Very funny," she said, swatting his arm lightly. "No. I'm finishing school. I've got a film studies program starting next semester, and maybe, just maybe, a part in something smaller, more... real. No armor. No stunt doubles. Just stories worth telling."

Anthony slumped dramatically into the seat across from them. "Great. So now I have to carry the franchise and do my own stunts."

"You'll survive," Mia teased. "Besides, you look great in fake bronze."

The door jingled again as Anna and Bennett walked in, waving before sliding into the booth. Anna plopped her backpack on the table. "Please tell me this isn't another meeting about thieves or explosions."

"Nope," Jack said, leaning back with a grin. "Tonight, we're only solving the mystery of who's paying for dinner."

Anthony lifted a hand. "Not it."

Mia crossed her arms. "You're wearing my face on a T-shirt. You're definitely paying."

Jack raised a finger like a referee calling time-out. "Relax, team. Already handled." He held up the menu for emphasis. "One extra-large Tiki Special, half pepperoni, half pineapple and sausage. On me."

Bennett grinned. "The detective strikes again."

As the server carried over steaming pizzas and clinking sodas, laughter filled the booth, the kind of laughter that came easily after everything they'd been through. The neon lights reflected in their glasses, painting the scene in pinks, greens, and purples.

Mia took a long sip of her soda and looked around the table, the friends who had become family. "You know," she said softly, "for a bunch of high-school kids, we've done alright."

Jack smiled, meeting her eyes. "Yeah," he said. "And something tells me this won't be our last mystery."

Anthony raised his slice in a toast. "To Mill Bay's finest."

"To the Gladiator Thief," Anna added.

"To surviving the movie business," Mia laughed.

Jack lifted his slice last. "And to pizza, our true reward."

They clinked slices together, the music from the jukebox swelling into a mellow tune. Outside, the lake shimmered under the fading sunset, and for one perfect moment, everything was still.

Pizza at the Tiki Club turned into an impromptu party that overflowed onto the boardwalk.

Jack's family beaming with pride. Even Georgia, normally too cool to care, admitted, "Okay, fine. You did something awesome."

For the first time in weeks, Jack could finally breathe.

Later that night, as the music faded and the crowd thinned, Jack stood on the dock overlooking Lake Naismith. The water shimmered under the stars, calm and endless.

"You really did it," Mia said, stepping beside him. "Took down a movie star."

Jack chuckled. "Yeah, not exactly how I planned to spend my summer."

Mia smiled. "Could've fooled me. You looked like a natural under those arena lights."

Jack turned to her, heart thudding. Without overthinking it, he leaned in and kissed her. It was brief but enough to leave the night glowing.

When they pulled apart, Mia smirked. "Not bad, Sawyer."

Before Jack could reply, his phone buzzed. Naomi Tanaka.

He sighed with a grinning at the timing of the call. He answered. "Hey, Naomi."

"Hey yourself," she said. "You ever think about coming to the big city? There's always another mystery waiting."

Jack smiled. "Tempting. But I think Mill Bay's got plenty to keep me busy."

Naomi laughed. "Suit yourself. But keep your phone on, I've got something interesting coming your way."

When the call ended, Jack pocketed the phone and looked back at Mia. "I think I'm done kissing my partners. Complicates the job."

She raised an eyebrow. "You sure about that?"

Jack hesitated, then grinned. "Okay... maybe one more time."

The next afternoon, the buzz from the movie's wrap party had finally started to fade. The sun shimmered off Lake Naismith as Jack leaned against the railing outside the Tiki Club, a can of root beer in his hand. Mia approached, holding an envelope.

"Delivery for our resident gladiator," she said with a smile, handing it over.

Jack opened it, half-expecting a note or another twist in their mystery. Instead, he found a neatly folded pay stub with his name on it, his official paycheck from *Gladiator Uprising.*

He blinked, a grin spreading across his face. "Guess we're professionals now."

Mia laughed. "Told you all that trident practice would pay off."

Jack looked at the check again, doing some quick math in his head. "Half's going straight into savings," he said. "For school."

Mia raised an eyebrow. "And the other half?"

Jack's smile softened. "A car. Something reliable but fun. I'm tired of bumming rides to class. And maybe a smartwatch for Georgia, so she can text me when I drop her off at swim lessons. She keeps pretending she's fine, but she still gets nervous before practice."

Mia leaned beside him on the railing, the sunlight catching in her hair. "You're a good brother, Jack Sawyer."

He shrugged. "Trying to be."

She nudged his shoulder. "For a guy who started his summer chasing a thief, you're ending it like a hero."

Jack chuckled. "Nah. Just a kid with a paycheck and a lot to figure out."

As laughter and music drifted from the Tiki Club, Jack gazed out over the lake. For once, the mystery was solved, the villain unmasked, and the world felt steady again.

But deep down, he knew peace never lasted long.

He was and always would be the Mill Bay Detective.

And somewhere out there, another mystery was already waiting.

EPILOGUE: NEW BEGINNINGS

The new school year at Mill Bay High began with a buzz that no homework or pep rally could top. Reading the first-day bulletin still made him double-check every line. Dyslexia didn't just disappear but neither did the determination it gave him. For Jack Sawyer, every mystery, every challenge, was just another way to prove that he could see what others missed. The hallways hummed with whispers, locker doors slamming in rhythm to the same name: Darius Slate.

Word was he'd cut a deal.

In exchange for exposing everyone who had helped him pull off the Gladiator Thief heists, from prop handlers to financial backers, he'd managed to dodge any real jail time. It was classic Darius, always landing on his feet, always spinning his story. Some said he'd even signed a tell-all deal before the ink on his confession was dry.

News reports confirmed that Marcus Trent and Broderick Johnson were both facing jail time for their roles in the Gladiator Thief robberies, but investigators hinted that Darius Slate's money and connections were still shielding them from the full consequences. Even behind bars, it seemed the star's influence reached further than justice liked to admit.

Jack just shook his head when he heard it. "The guy's addicted to attention," he muttered to Anthony. "Even when he's not acting, he's performing."

Life in Mill Bay was quieter now, or at least as quiet as it ever got. The Gladiator Uprising set had long been dismantled, leaving behind only rumors and a few battered props floating around local memorabilia shops. Still, every so often, Jack caught tourists taking selfies by the old training grounds, pretending to wield invisible tridents.

After school one day, Jack spotted Mia talking to Naomi on her tablet, deep in conversation. Mia had decided to stay in Mill Bay for the last of her classes and would be writing her final exams soon. They looked serious. Jack recognized that look, the spark that came before a new mystery.

"Top secret project," Anthony said, appearing beside him with a grin. "Word is they're both working on something in Mill Bay. Studio hush-hush. Classified, according to Mia."

Jack raised an eyebrow. "Knowing those two? It's probably part detective work, part world-saving mission."

Anthony laughed. "You thinking what I'm thinking?"

"That we should probably stay out of it?" Jack said.

Anthony smirked. "Exactly. At least until it gets

interesting."

Later that night Jack sat alone at his desk, the same small one that used to hold nothing but homework and graphic novels. Now, his old laptop glowed softly in the dark, the cursor blinking on a blank web page.

He stared at the words he'd just typed:

Mill Bay Detective Agency.

Jack leaned back in his chair, smiling. It sounded bold, maybe even a little ridiculous, but after a summer of chasing thieves, dodging danger, and outsmarting movie stars, it didn't feel impossible.

He started filling out the basics: a short description, an email address, and a logo. He even set up an account on social media "@millbaydetective: No mystery too small."

The door creaked open behind him. Georgia peeked in, still wearing her new smartwatch. "You're up late again," she said.

Jack smiled. "Just setting up something new."

She padded over and squinted at the screen. "You're really doing it, huh?"

"Yeah," Jack said, hitting "Publish." "Time to make it official."

Georgia grinned. "Can I be your assistant?"

Jack laughed. "We'll see. For now, get some sleep, junior detective."

As the page went live, Jack stared at the glowing screen one last time feeling confident that there isn't much he and his friends can't do when they work together.

BOOKS BY THIS AUTHOR

The Maui Mystery

When Jack Sawyer wins a science fair with his groundbreaking app for students with dyslexia, he thinks his biggest challenge will be presenting at the prestigious International Young Innovators Fair in Maui. But the tropical paradise takes a mysterious turn when the event's organizer, Dr. Grant Sterling, vanishes—and Jack's new friend, Naomi, becomes the target of a high-tech theft.

Teaming up, the unlikely duo uncovers a tangled web of corporate greed, environmental secrets, and stolen innovations. From secret jungle labs to stormy chases through the Hawaiian docks, Jack and Naomi must use their wits, courage, and cutting-edge tech to uncover the truth and bring a mastermind to justice.

Packed with thrilling twists, humor, and heart, The Maui Mystery is a gripping adventure about friendship, ingenuity, and daring to stand up for what's right—even when the odds are stacked against you.

33233407R00068